G R JORDAN

Frostbite

A Contessa Munroe Mystery

First published by Carpetless Publishing 2021

First edition

ISBN: 978-1-914073-22-9

This book was professionally typeset on Reedsy.
Find out more at reedsy.com

Skiing is the only sport where you spend an arm and a leg to break an arm and a leg.

ANONYMOUS

Contents

Foreword

This story is set in a fictious resort amongst the french ski resorts. Any persons named are entirely fictional, as are the events in the resort and on the snow. I'm not sure if I wish some of these people were real but I do like the idea of a warm fire amidst the biting cold of the snow.

Acknowledgement

To Susan, Jean and Rosemary for your work in bringing this novel to completion, your time and effort is deeply appreciated.

Novels by G R Jordan

The Highlands and Islands Detective series (Crime)

1. Water's Edge
2. The Bothy
3. The Horror Weekend
4. The Small Ferry
5. Dead at Third Man
6. The Pirate Club
7. A Personal Agenda
8. A Just Punishment
9. The Numerous Deaths of Santa Claus
10. Our Gated Community
11. The Satchel
12. Culhwch Alpha

The Contessa Munroe Mysteries (Cozy Mystery)

1. Corpse Reviver
2. Frostbite
3. Cobra's Fang

The Patrick Smythe Series (Crime)

1. The Disappearance of Russell Hadleigh

2. The Graves of Calgary Bay
3. The Fairy Pools Gathering

Austerley & Kirkgordon Series (Fantasy)

1. Crescendo!
2. The Darkness at Dillingham
3. Dagon's Revenge
4. Ship of Doom

Supernatural and Elder Threat Assessment Agency (SETAA) Series (Fantasy)

1. Scarlett O'Meara: Beastmaster

Island Adventures Series (Cosy Fantasy Adventure)

1. Surface Tensions

Dark Wen Series (Horror Fantasy)

1. The Blasphemous Welcome
2. The Demon's Chalice

Chapter 1

Catriona Cullodena Monroe was in a good mood. Despite having had to wake Tiff up that morning and haul her out of the door into the waiting taxi before jumping onto the plane, Cat was feeling well disposed towards her niece. Over the last week, Tiff had been in all sorts of excitement, as the time to go to the slopes came closer. Cat had never witnessed Tiff on a snowboard, but by all accounts, she knew how to handle one and her niece had told Cat that without a doubt, if she could find a half-pipe, she would show Cat some tricks.

Cat was not so keen on the snow, but the resort they had picked seemed highly exclusive, with a chalet all to themselves, in a small commune away from the usual ski crowds. It wasn't that Cat was particularly a toff and deemed herself above others, but right now she wanted some space. They had tried previously to get away on a cruise ship in the Northern waters, but things had gone astray. Catriona was not looking for excitement. All she wanted was a small chalet she could base herself in, a roaring fire, and possibly a few drinks. If Tiff had the benefit of different snow games to entertain her, then all the better.

The last part of their trip had possibly been the worst with a road that ran here and there, climbing up the mountainside far from the rest of civilization. Catriona had thought—incorr ectly, as it turned out—that they would be on some sort of ski lift or cable car up to the commune. The lack of one up to this group of chalets maybe deterred unwelcome snoopers, people wanting to see how the other half lived. After inheriting money, or rather being paid off by Luigi's family after his untimely death, Catriona was a woman of leisure, free to wander the world, and she'd taken it upon herself to bring Tiff with her.

Tiffany Monroe, her brother's daughter, was not easy to get along with. They said she was somewhere on the spectrum, and in Cat's mind, Tiff lived in a partial world of her own, occasionally drifting away to it before returning to this world. That being said, she was incredibly astute of mind and she saw things Cat failed to spot. However, she could take a good deal of lessons from her aunt as to how to deal with social situations. Tiff detested speaking to people, preferring to shove on her earphones rather than engage in polite conversation. Catriona, on the other hand, loved to watch and then engage people.

She'd been watching their driver, a rather stout young man, possibly twenty, who seemed more than capable of handling a wheel. The road up to the commune required a four by four, and every now and again, Cat would be thrown here and there by the bumps in the road. Yet the young man was never fazed by any of it, turning around and smiling broadly at Tiffany and Catriona whenever the jolt was just that bit too severe. Outside the car window, Catriona saw fields of white with trees dotted over the mountainside. This was more like it, up and away from it all, into the wild cold. There was no reason here to go on an excursion. Rather she could wake, stay by the fire, maybe even ski with Tiff a little if she wanted to bond with her a bit more, but otherwise, enjoy the food, seek out company, and happily drown whatever sorrows came to mind.

They rounded a small copse of trees, and a large log structure appeared, vast compared to any normal chalet, and with a driveway neatly cleared of snow so that her driver was able to position the car at the entrance. Catriona tutted as Tiff jumped out on her side, not waiting for the driver to open the door, but the man knew his duty and Catriona gladly took his hand as he helped her and advised her to watch her step on the slippery ground. Cat felt she should be in some sort of elegant ballgown as she approached her large wooden cabin, but instead, she wore a pair of designer jeans and a large beige jumper. Her jacket was around her shoulders and a pair of sunglasses had been lifted off her nose onto the top of her head. She wasn't here to impress. She was here to relax, and she smiled as she heard Tiff excitedly urging her driver to open the boot so she could retrieve her snowboard.

'Let the man bring the rest, Tiffany. It's what he does. Let's get inside and we'll find out where we're staying.' Catriona turned and saw her niece hugging her snowboard, wrapped up in a special cover. Tiff's long hair run down her back despite being tied in a ponytail, and her normally impassive face was beaming. It was a joy to see because the girl was usually so hard to read, so difficult to engage, but now, she seemed like she could be ready to be the heart and soul of the party. Maybe that was too much to expect, but nonetheless, Cat had a feeling that this time in the mountains was going to be good.

Striding up the steps into the log cabin, the entrance was opened for Cat by a man rather casually dressed for a doorman. From behind the counter, a man raced forward, giving a casual wave and bidding Cat a welcome in French. Her French wasn't particularly good, but the man was quite fluent. However, her face must have given away that she wasn't completely understanding everything as he quickly changed into English.

'Welcome. Welcome. My name is Denis, Denis Dupont, and I'm here to make your stay with us comfortable. Apart from the staff who come in to clean, there are only two of us here, myself, and behind the counter, you can see Coralie, our resident ski instructor, if any of you require any help.'

'Well, that will be for Cat then,' said Tiff. 'Do you have a half-pipe?'

'I believe there is a small tricks park,' said Denis. 'You will need to speak to Coralie about that. She does get quite worried about some people who like to, how you say, have a go, but if you can show her you're proficient, then you're more than welcome to use it.'

'Oh, don't worry, Mr. Dupont. Tiffany's quite proficient.'

'Denis, please. May I say it's delightful to have a Contessa here.'

Cat had almost forgotten she was a Contessa, but now she was here, everything was sublime. You could feel like you were one of the jet set, but she almost felt quite ordinary as well. She didn't like her title because some people started to get very silly and began bowing, as if she was some sort of royalty. Well, maybe technically, she was some sort of royalty, but not the kind that should be bowed to. As long as they attended to her needs, opened doors, cooked food for her, sorted out her bed and clothes, then Cat didn't need bowed to. She just needed life's trivial matters taken care of.

Denis escorted the pair over to the counter where he ran through several security issues about the compound they were to stay in. Compound seemed such an awkward word to

Cat, but she could not come up with something better at that moment. There was a total of six chalets beyond the rather large central log cabin. *Cabin was the wrong word though,* thought Cat. *Yes, it was made of logs, but the size of it compared to a normal house made it more like a central meeting facility.* There was a small restaurant or dining area near a common area, the centre piece of which was a large fire which had crackling logs on it. Doors were signposted for ski equipment, a gym and even a swimming pool, all of which brought delight to Cat's face. This is what she wanted. Somewhere away from it all with no people.

Denis explained that the facilities were open 24/7 to be used as and when with only himself and Coralie there to assist. Guests were at liberty to just come and go as they please. He handed over a buzzer, as he called it. *More of a pager,* thought Cat, something with which he could be contacted at any time, day or night. In fairness, the man seemed to be rabbiting on, and Cat detected a nervousness in him, but she was in a good mood, and rather than criticize his professionalism, she simply put out her hand. When he took it, she shook it gently.

'Everything seems to be very much in order, Denis. I'm sure we're going to be incredibly happy here. If you can just point us out to our chalet, I think we'll go and unpack. Simply tell our driver where to go.'

'Indeed,' said Denis. 'You're right at the top, and I hope that's no inconvenience. It's not a long walk, maybe some 200 metres, but I'll make sure that your bags are taken up there right away. If you just wait here, I'll sort that before coming to escort you up there myself.'

Cat turned around and smiled at Tiff, who was still clutching her board, her eyes wandering around the building.

'Are you okay?' asked Cat.

'He hasn't mentioned the slopes yet. I want to go and see the slopes.'

'We can get changed as soon as we get up there. Let's get in, get unpacked, and then away you go. You know I'm not a great skier, but if you want me with you, I'm happy to come with you until you find everywhere. I know it sometimes takes you a bit to gel in with people.'

Tiff gave a look as if Cat had said the most ridiculous thing in the world. 'Why do you say that? I haven't got a problem. It's just sometimes other people have a problem with me.' Cat thought about arguing, but instead merely smiled and reiterated that she'd be happy to escort her niece out to the slopes until she could find her way around.

There was a loud crash as the front door was opened, and Cat saw a young woman surrounded by at least six or seven people. She was dark skinned, but Cat thought her flesh was the most perfect shade and it was smooth. She could tell because the woman's arms were bare despite the cold outside. Maybe the woman had jumped out of a limo, but her black hair with long ringlets fell in a wave behind her. She had eyelashes that for the modern woman seemed perfect, long, well-developed, but obviously not real.

Catriona never enhanced her eyelashes because they were so large to begin with. Some people said that was what first grabbed them about her, her eyes. Catriona was not someone who used makeup extensively, but the woman who had entered knew how to use it. Cat was quite taken aback by her overall image. Before she could say anything, the woman tore right through the building and out of the rear door, surrounded by six or seven hangers-on. They all looked trendy, certainly well up with the times, in a way that Cat always failed to do. There was plenty of laughing and joking as they all milled along together, and it brought Cat a warm sensation. This is what she wanted, people being themselves, not bothering anyone else.

Denis was taking his time with the baggage, and rather than get frustrated, Catriona thought she might pick up a drink while she was waiting. She looked over to the bar area beyond the large central fire and saw a couple almost leaning on it. One was a rather bland looking girl, but she was really tall, possibly six foot. Whereas she wore a rather drab blue blouse and jeans and had a face that spoke of concern for the man beside her, he was dressed in a rather light shirt and snappy pair of trousers. His shoes were bright red, and Cat was not sure they matched, for he certainly struck a figure. The man was waving his arms around while the woman ran her hand through his brown hair. Cat watched him pick up a cocktail shaker before reaching for several bottles from behind the bar. The woman clearly was not amused and began shaking her head furiously at him. Undaunted, the man continued to open the bottles before pouring a mix into a cocktail shaker, topping it up with some ice and then shaking it right in front of her face. Cat saw the woman's foot stamp the ground.

'Right here, right in front of me, you would do it in my face.'

'We're here to enjoy ourselves. Lighten up, Alice. Just because you have issues at home, don't bring them here with us. We're here to enjoy ourselves. Come on.'

'I swear on my father's life, Kyle Cobbler, if you put that drink to your lips, I'll walk away from here.'

'Just because your father died a pisshead doesn't mean I will. Besides, there's nothing like a nice bit of frostbite when you're right in the cold.'

Catriona saw the man take the drink in his hand, and she recognized the colour of it. It was indeed a frostbite, and despite the scene before her, part of her wanted to walk over and ask if could he make her one as well? She turned to Tiff.

'Do you see those two over there? Seems a bit steep, doesn't it? Bit full on.'

'How far away do you think the half-pipe is?'

'Did you hear what I said, Tiff? Those two over there, did you hear them arguing?'

'What did Denis say the woman's name was? The ski instructor—Cecily?'

'Coralie. He said she was called Coralie. Don't be bothering her too quick. She's got everyone to look after. Besides, you're not looking for lessons. You're just trying to show off.'

'No, I'm not,' said Tiff. 'We do need to get going. Where's the luggage?'

'Just calm down. Just calm down. We'll be there soon enough.'

Cat heard the thwack of a hand slapping someone's cheek, and she flicked her head back round to the bar where the couple now stood in much more aggressive stances. Clearly, the woman had slapped the man, his drink having spilled on to the bar. He was trying to stand up to her, but at six foot, she was always going to tower over him.

'Just don't come near me. That's it. Just don't come near me. You don't expect anything from me.'

As the woman walked away, the man shouted after her. 'Was getting nothing anyway, might as well get pissed. Anybody else want one?' he shouted to the room in general.

Cat felt bad when something inside her said, *Yes, me.* Instead, she had the good sense to turn away and pretend she was talking to Tiff. Tiffany, on the other hand, simply looked over Cat's shoulder and stared at the man. 'You'd probably want a drink, wouldn't you?' said Tiff.

'Not now. Besides, look, there's our luggage. Come on.' Cat took Tiff by the hand and dragged her over toward Denis, who was ushering their driver through the building and out towards the back door.

'Is that man all right over there?' Cat asked Denis.

'Oh, the students, the students,' he said. 'Oh, they shout here, they shout there. I say to them, this is a quiet resort. This is a resort where people relax, get along, come together, nice chat, nice talk, but no, they have to shout and get on. I don't know how they afford to be here. They're just students.'

'They're all sons and daughters of somebody,' said Cat. 'Maybe that somebody has money. Well, don't worry, Denis, it hasn't bothered me, just giving it a bit of spice, especially after that gorgeous woman walked in with the other group of people.'

'Jodie,' he said. 'Yes, she's a French singing star. Maybe you've heard?'

Cat shook her head and then turned to Tiff to see if she knew the woman.

'Seen her on Instagram, Facebook, something like that,' said Tiff. 'All about makeup, clothes and fashion. Looked boring.'

Cat shook her head. She was not sure Tiff was not making it all up and had never seen the woman. 'Never mind, Denis. Lead on. I want to see my chalet.' With that, Denis nodded and guided them out of the rear door, but across from them, Tiff could see a girl looking back in through the windows of the main area cabin where Tiff imagined the man was mixing himself another drink.

Chapter 2

Catriona thought that Tiff might at the very least have stopped to unpack her bags, but as it turned out, Denis had not even left by the time Tiff was heading out the door looking for Coralie. Cat smiled pleasantly at Denis and told him not to worry, that her niece was just simply excited, and in truth, she was. When Cat had mentioned about going skiing, Tiff, at first, had almost looked the other way because she was having one of those days when she didn't communicate with people. But the following day, she'd been all over her aunt, insisting on details about the possible slopes and stunt parks that may be close by. Cat had no idea about any of that side of things. All she knew was it was a resort that was set away from everywhere else and she shouldn't be disturbed but still have some interesting people to speak to.

And she hoped this time that was the case. Last time, she'd become embroiled in a possible murder, which then turned into an actual murder. It was only the combination of her doggedness and Tiff's cleverness that saw the day through. Although in reality, she was still wondering how they did that, but this time would be different. This time, she was here to enjoy herself.

Once Denis had left, Cat opened the case in her bedroom

and unpacked, placing everything in her drawers. She could've asked someone to do it, but really, this was a sort of therapy as well. She struggled to have a home anymore. Yes, there was a flat back in Scotland she retreated to occasionally, but more and more, she was on the move around the world. So, when she was stopping somewhere for several weeks, to unpack meant to lay down her standards on a place, acknowledge it as being hers for that time. Of course, Tiff didn't need any of that. She was out the door and so Cat ended up unpacking Tiffany's clothes as well. But she didn't mind. Nothing could knock her at the moment. This was a sort of bliss.

The journey had been tiring and so Cat slipped out of her clothes and into a warm bath. In truth, it was more of a mini spa than a bath and Cat thought she could probably swim in it. But the water was warm, the bubbles were good, and she was able to pour herself a glass of wine, sipping it as she lay there enjoying the pampering.

One thing that she definitely wasn't going to be doing this time around was try to attract any men. The one man that was after her last time on their rather strange excursion to the northern waters had turned out to be quite a cad. So, this time, it would be just her and Tiff. Yes, she'd mingle. Yes, she'd talk and mix, but she wasn't looking for anything beyond that.

It was funny because Luigi hadn't been dead that long and some people would say she was rather quick to start seeking out others, but Cat knew herself. She needed that close contact. She was that sort of person. But maybe she'd been too quick, maybe she needed to learn to slow down a little. Well, certainly here was a good place to start.

But something was missing, and Cat knew what it was. She hauled herself out of the bath, quickly running into the bedroom where she spied a speaker and dragged it into the bathroom. She attached her phone to it via Bluetooth and within a few minutes, she was listening to one of her favourite singers. Some people thought Ella Fitzgerald was a little old school, but when she wanted to relax, Cat found that a bit of old school soothed the soul. Now that the tracks were playing, she stepped back into the bath, let herself slide down underneath the bubbles, her mouth barely clearing the water, and lay there as her hair floated by the side of her.

If Tiff had wanted to make sure that Cat was aware she was in the chalet, she couldn't have done a better job. Catriona thought the door had come off its hinges, it was closed so loudly and the thud of Tiff running through the chalet, crying out Cat's name, broke an incredibly peaceful moment. Sometimes, she was like a little kid, just charging around, saying what she wanted.

'What's the matter, Tiff? I'm in the bath. Can't it wait? I've just got under the water. I'm trying to relax.'

There was no answer until the door was flung open and Tiff stood, looking at her aunt with no sign of shame or apology for breaking the quiet.

'Do come in then,' said Cat. But clearly, it was going straight over Tiff's head.

'It's all a bit weird.' This was a standard Tiff comment, one where she expected you to understand the context and the actual elements of what she was talking about when she'd given you no clue whatsoever.

'What's weird? Do you mean like the ski park or the slopes?'

'No,' said Tiff, again giving Catriona the feeling that she should've understood. 'He is.'

'He? Who? Denis?'

'No, not Denis. Not him, he's okay. The other man.'

'What other man? You mean the guy with the drink? His girl slapped him.'

'No, the other guy.'

'Right, you're going to have to help me, Tiff. Basically, we came up in the 4X4 and I know the driver. And then there was Denis, and there was the man at the bar. There were a couple of people in the entourage, but other than that, I don't know who. Was it one of them?'

'No,' said Tiff again rather dismissively.

'Well, then who?'

'The man with the binoculars.'

'What man with the binoculars?' This drove Cat mad. All the time, Tiff would go on about stuff as if Cat knew what she was talking about. Yet, there was no reason for her to expect you to. 'What man with binoculars?' said Cat. 'Where is he?'

'He's outside.'

Catriona instantly flung her hands across her chest. Then felt rather stupid for doing so. 'Right outside our chalet?'

'No,' said Tiff, 'He's not looking in here. He's not trying to get a peep at you. Why would he want to get a peep at you?'

Tiff was incredibly good at delivering a backhanded compliment or insulting you by trying to deny something you've said. Whatever she said back, you felt as low as possible generally and she had no idea she'd even done it.

Cat thought that many men would fight to get a good look at her in the bath. Then she realized what a horrible feeling that actually was. She shook her head to clear any ideas about people looking here, there, or wherever, and whether she was of an appropriate level of attractiveness to do that.

Cat went back to the main problem. 'What man and where?'

'I told you it's the man with the binoculars. He's on the other side, looking over at one of the other chalets. He's hidden behind one of the trees. Don't worry—he didn't see me.'

'That's good. I wouldn't like to think somebody thought you were spying on them when they were spying on someone else. What's the big problem, anyway?' Tiff stepped over and picked up a towel before turning and holding it out for Catriona. 'I'm not coming out of here to go and see some man with binoculars looking at something,' said Cat.

'You don't understand. I think he's ogling, staring at a woman.'

'Why? Did you see him stare at a woman? Did you see actually who he was looking at or what he was looking at?'

'No,' said Tiff, 'but it's obvious, isn't it? A man with binoculars out in the snow here; he must be looking at a woman.'

'He could be looking at anyone,' said Cat. 'I think it's best if I just stay here.'

'No,' said Tiff, 'you're coming out. I need you to come out with me now.'

'No, I'm not.'

'When are you coming out? Tell me when you're coming out. You need to come out now,' cried Tiff.

This was typical. Once Tiff got something in her head that you had to do, you had to do it. There was no fair play involved. It was just what Tiff wanted.

'Wait, I'm coming. Give me that towel and give me ten minutes.'

'Ten minutes,' said Tiff. 'He could be gone by then. Come on, hurry up.' For a moment Cat thought that Tiff was going to dry her. But thankfully she handed over the towel and left, leaving Catriona to dry herself. Her hair could do with a brush through but Cat knew Tiff would not be long before she would be back into the bathroom. Cat dried quickly, dressed, and threw on a bobble hat and a coat before trudging out into the snow with Tiff.

The chalet was located at the top of the commune and to the left and right Cat saw two other chalets followed by another pair, slightly lower down. There was one more slightly set off to the left, making a total of six.

'Where is he?' asked Cat.

'This way,' said Tiff. They started trudging through the snow, but the girls were well equipped. Cat walked along in her snowshoes and was wrapped up in a large jacket that looked more like a warm duvet. Tiff was dressed in her full snowboard outfit and she looked like some competitor from the slopes. However, she was also very brightly coloured.

Cat was wondering how they were going to sneak about with the pair of them looking like some sort of winter Mardi gras festival. Tiff led the way around the back of one of the chalets and then out towards the woods. Once she stepped inside the tree line, about some twenty metres, Tiff cut back down the slope. Then turned back towards the commune within five metres of where the tree line broke. She stopped Cat and pointed.

'There he is peering, still looking. What's he doing? He's definitely up to something.'

'He has a pair of binoculars and he's looking. The man could well be looking at birds or whatever.'

'Can you hear any birds here?'

'Yes, I can hear the occasional bird,' said Cat.

'I think he's up to something. I think maybe he's targeting

someone.'

'Previously, it looked like he was going to be a voyeur, but now you've got him down as ready to kill people. I think we're getting a bit excited. Is this because of what happened on the boat?'

Tiff shook her head. 'Don't,' she said, 'I'm telling you something's not right there and I think he's watching a woman. We should go up and tell him off.'

'We are going nowhere,' said Catriona. 'We've just arrived and I'm not pissing off somebody already. What we'll do is walk over there close to him.'

'You can talk to him,' said Tiff.

'I am not talking to him. We're going to stay well clear of him, and we're going to make sure we don't get seen by him. Then we'll have a look and see what he's looking at. If it turns out to be a woman, then we'll start thinking about what we do.'

Tiff didn't seem convinced, but she let Cat lead the way round before the pair of them hollered up again behind some trees.

'Look,' said Tiff. 'What's he watching?'

Catriona looked along the line of the side of the man and saw one of the chalets. At the large window stood a woman dressed in rather innocuous and normal everyday clothes, but she did seem to be alone.

'I told you,' said Tiff, 'like he's spying on her. He's waiting to see if she gets undressed.'

'She's in the lounge,' said Catriona. 'Why is she going to start taking clothes off? No, I think he just must be interested.'

'Interested, that's what they say about all murder victims. That the other people were interested in them. I think we all know what he's interested in her for?'

'You don't know that. Besides, we'll just keep an eye on him. Maybe we'll mention it to Denis, but he could also be looking at birds.'

'No, he's not,' said Tiff. 'Don't be ridiculous.'

'Yes, he may be.' Catriona pointed to some feathered friends that were sitting up on the chalet. 'Maybe it's those that he's looking at—maybe he's a bird spotter.'

'It doesn't look like a twitcher to me,' said Tiff. 'I think we should go in and say to her.'

'No,' said Cat. 'I'm not starting off this holiday by chasing off everybody else that's here. No, we don't do that. We'll just sit and watch him for a bit? See what he does.' The man in question was dressed in black, although the trousers looked quite thick and the jacket certainly appeared to be warm enough. He had a black beanie on as well, and Cat wondered why he wore such a combination. She started to make her way forward, moving in behind a tree each time, before checking ahead to see what was coming her way. Soon, the two women had acquired a position that allowed them to get an even better view of the man.

'He's looking at the woman,' said Tiff.

'You're right,' said Catriona. 'He is looking in that direction, but we're not going to face off with him.'

'Why? Why on earth not?' said Tiff.

'Because look at us; what would we do if we go up to him and he is some sort of serial killer? We'd be dead in no time. Are you going to defend me against him? No, and I'm not going to be able to defend myself. No, we're leaving him alone,' said Cat.

'That's quite a cowardly attitude to take. Well, I'm going to say something,' said Tiff.

Catriona reached forward and grabbed her hand. Just then the man put his binoculars down and started to walk away.

'I think I'll mention it to Denis at some point,' said Cat. 'It's best not to worry everybody; he might have some perfectly good reason for what he's doing.' Tiff seemed to be somewhat appeased, but she told Cat that she was not heading to the slopes tonight. Instead, the pair walked the short distance back to the chalet. Once inside, Cat decided to get back into the bath as she was feeling the chill. By the time she made it to the bathroom, she realized that Tiff was already in there and under the water.

'That's just dandy. I think you just put that guy over there to get me out of the bath.'

'What?' said Tiff. Cat shook her head. There was no point pursuing it further with Tiff; she never got the irony.

Chapter 3

'So, when do we eat in this place?' said Tiff. Contrary to her earlier statement, Tiff had made an excursion out on the slopes. Having stepped inside the door, she placed her snowboard to one side, causing Cat to give a shake of the head.

'Are you going to leave that there? It probably should be outside. Otherwise, it's going to drip wet everywhere.'

'I'll put it in the bath then. You can shift it out if you want another soak. Either that or I'll pop it down to the main chalet, but I'm starving, Cat. When do we eat?'

'Well, they said we can eat up here. I mean, there is some food in the fridge and stuff. We can make our own, but apparently, we can pop down to the main building as well. They say Denis can cook.'

'Well, I'm not cooking. Let's go down. I'm just going to get out of the suit first.' Catriona nodded and went back to the book she was reading. For most of the afternoon, Cat had sat and not thought about the strange man looking with his binoculars at the woman in the other chalet. She did, however, close the curtains to make sure no one could look in. Admittedly, she did feel a bit daft. Maybe it was a bit of paranoia, but she didn't want to be ogled, not from a distance by a man dressed in black. He didn't even look at all shapely.

It took Tiff over half an hour to get changed and when she came to the lounge, Cat insisted she went to the bathroom to have a shower. 'There's no use you walking in here, smelling like something. You've been out boarding. Did you find the halfpipe, by the way?'

Tiff shook her head. 'No, and I didn't find that Coralie person either, but there were some good slopes I went on. They actually have a couple of ski lifts, and our slope's quite private. It's not the most difficult, but then again, I guess they keep the really proper ones for the masses.'

'We'll find out tonight,' said Cat. 'Now get in that shower.'

'All right. If you insist.' It was another half hour before Tiff returned, but this time she was dressed in a sloppy jumper and jeans, her hair hanging right in front of her face as if she didn't want anyone to see her. Together, the pair put on coats and trudged down to the main building, where they saw a number of people inside. Cat recognized the arguing couple from earlier on, along with a number of other young people. There was a family group with two kids, boys by the look of it, and in one corner, she also saw the man who had been dressed in black. Maybe this was the time to go and speak to him about what he was doing. Although, better not with Tiff. She might be a bit too direct with the questions.

Striding through the door, Cat caught the eye of Denis, who gave a nod and raced over. When she asked for food, Denis produced a couple of menus and then quickly made his way back to the counter, and then through a small door at the back. Sitting down beside the large, raging fire, just across from the bar, Cat told Tiff to hold their place and make up her mind about food and Cat quietly sauntered over to the man in black at the rear.

'Have you just arrived too?' asked Cat, giving a friendly smile. The man shook his head. 'I'm sorry, I didn't catch your name,' said Cat. Again, there was nothing from the man. 'Oh, I'm sorry. I haven't said my own name. I'm Catriona and that's my niece, Tiff. Who are you?'

Like a captain on deck, the man turned slowly, gazing at Catriona as if she was some piece of driftwood on its way past. 'Jobert,' he said very deliberately. 'Bertrand Jobert, and I am on my own. That is how I like it.' With that, he turned away, leaving Cat to wonder if her personable face had so turned off the man. Unfazed, she strode over to a couple by the bar.

'Hello,' said the man, 'I'm John, John Roberts. You look like you could do with a cocktail.'

Cat's eyes lit up, 'Always ready for one of those,' she said. 'Catriona.'

'Ah, the Contessa,' said the woman. 'I'm Celia Roberts, John's wife. Do you like your skiing? I take it that's why you're here?'

Cat shook her head. 'No, my niece over there, she's the snowboarder. She likes to half-pipe and all that sort of thing. Whatever that means.' The woman looked slightly disappointed. 'Well, she'd go out with you if you want,' said Cat. The woman smiled somewhat but then turned away. After a few moments, she slowly steered towards Tiff by the fire. Catriona wondered what sort of response she would get, but she never got the chance to find out as John engaged her in conversation. 'John Roberts, and excuse my wife. Do you like Contessa or is it Catriona?'

'Always Catriona. In fact, Cat, John. I'm here to be away from it all. I don't want people making a fuss. It's not as if I'm proper royalty, anyway.'

'You have a title, so you're proper. That's what I always find. Anyway, I can't ski either. I'm just here for the wildlife. Time to get away from it all. See, well, she'll be off on down those slopes, like anything, but I want peace and quiet. Anyway, what do you like to drink? I'm quite a good hand at making some of these things.'

'Can you do a frostbite?' said Cat. 'Quite appropriate really? Isn't it?'

'Damn right it is.' John looked over at the group of students in the far corner. 'Anyone for cocktails,' he shouted. A number of arms went up and shouts of hurrah. 'Looks like I'm making a good selection then.' Cat smiled and pulled herself up onto a seat at the bar while John stepped behind it. He was quite a dab hand, shaking this and that, and he poured Catriona's cocktail first.

'Have a taste of that and tell me what you think.'

Catriona let the liquid fall down her throat. There was a bit of a kick to it, quite punchy. 'You'll do me but pour us another one before you send it over to them.'

'Oh, good stuff. Don't take this wrong, girl, but it'll be nice to have somebody to drink a few with. The missus isn't like that, but I hope you won't mind me bothering you for a drink every now and again. Nothing else, nothing else, maybe just a bit of good conversation.'

Cat tried to place the accent and was sure it was somewhere like Yorkshire and had that northern English feel about it.

'Anyway,' said John, 'you sound very Italian.'

'Scottish through and through, I'm afraid. My husband was the Italian.'

'Husband?' said John in shock. 'You look too young to have had a husband; divorced, I take it?'

'Widowed! Widowed too young, but that's that, and here I am.'

'Well, a pleasure to meet you, Contessa. You drink that down while I take these over to the other group.'

Cat turned to watch John delicately carry a tray over, piled high with a number of cocktails. The student party reached forward, each grabbing eagerly, and she noticed that the couple who were arguing earlier on were still at it, albeit in a quieter form. The six-foot girl didn't go near the cocktails and seemed to be sipping something like hot chocolate. Meanwhile, Denis came out to get Catriona's order, complete with a little flip pad and pen.

'Anything will do really,' said Cat; 'whatever you're making, some stew or that. Something nice and warm. I'll get that for Tiff too. If you go and ask her, she'll be funny and she'll ask for all sorts of things and then doesn't eat them. Whatever's good, Denis.'

The man looked almost crestfallen, as if he wanted to do something better, but he nodded politely and walked off. John had returned by this point, and Catriona saw other people arriving.

'Do you know that Jodie?' said Cat.

'You want to meet her?' asked John. 'One of these modern singers. Elvis is gone as far as I'm concerned, and that's about it.' He gave a laugh, 'But she usually has a lot of people around her, I see she's coming in on her own at the moment. I think sometimes they clear off or they get told to buzz off and let her be. She's a bit of a strange one, quite highly strung. Had the odd tizzy and that, but she's all right. You know, I've seen worse.'

'What about those students?' asked Cat. 'They seem to be a

lively bunch.'

'Oh, very lively. Especially those two there; have you seen them arguing? That's Alice and Kyle, and they're at that constantly. We can hear them from our chalet sometimes. In fact, a couple of days ago, I went over and had a word. Debbie, the girl at the back, the blonde one, she's the one paying for the trip. Quite surprised they were here really, a bunch of students, but Debbie's father has a bit of money from what I hear. That's Sarah with her, the brunette, the small one. Alan beside her, he's a bit thin on top. I think you might be slightly older than him, a mature student maybe, thirty-years-old.'

'The last of those, Derek, he's a bit strange. A bit of something around the eyes, never really looks at you when you talk to him. I'm also not sure how well they know him, but who knows. Other than that, it's nice and quiet around here, the scenery's unbelievable. Denis and Coralie look after us very well. And I don't mind saying, I wouldn't mind going skiing with Coralie.'

Cat looked at the man. *What a saucy old fool.* In these days and time, she probably should be a little shocked, but she wasn't. Maybe he was inappropriate, or was it incredibly good humour? It was strange how that happened. There were other people she thought could make a comment like that and she would feel quite threatened, but not him, not this John character. Maybe it was the Northern accent that did it. Cat noticed Jodie coming towards them, and she seemed a little upset.

'They haven't come back yet. Have you seen them, John, have you seen any of them?'

'No, and none of the vehicles have come back yet. Were you expecting them already? Surely, they were giving you a little space. Oh, by the way, can I introduce Contessa Catriona, or Cat?'

The woman barely looked at her, but now close up, Cat could see that perfect skin she had admired earlier. The girl was truly lovely, and Cat felt a slight jealousy because she could never fit into the outfit that the woman was wearing. So very glamorous while wearing something routine—how did they do that? Cat always felt when she dressed up, she looked like someone who had made an effort, but this girl, she just looked like this was what she wore all the time. Cat was more at home in jeans and a t-shirt, anyway.

'Here,' said Cat, lifting over a cocktail to Jodie. The girl took it without a thank you and started to drink it while looking around, and then she tore off in a completely different direction.

'A bit strange,' said Cat. 'Not very communicative.'

'You get like that,' said John, 'or so I'm told. You get like that when everyone's running around after you; maybe she doesn't really have a care for anyone else. Maybe she's never had to, maybe she's never—'

The lights inside the building all went out, leaving the fire in the centre of the room as the only thing going, but because of its vast size, everyone still had plenty of light to see by. Cat waited, almost anticipating the lights coming back on, but there was nothing. The students started to laugh and joke amongst themselves, but John looked a little concerned.

'I hope that's not what I think it is,' he said. 'We don't want a power cut up here; otherwise, we're going to be on ordinary fire heating. I know each chalet has got a nice big one, but that's a bit much really, isn't it? I wonder what's happening. I'm sure Denis will be out in a minute.'

It was five minutes before Denis was out with his torch, and running around, he gave a brief apology to the guests before disappearing through another door on the other side of the hall. Returning some two minutes later, he waved his arms for attention from all the guests.

'I'm sorry to say, there appears to be a power cut, and it must be further down because it's not come from here. However, I have most of the food cooked, so I will serve it, and if we stay in here, there's plenty of light from the fire. I will accompany people back tonight and get fires lit in the chalets if the power hasn't come back on. If we build the fires up, we should be warm enough; the chalets are well insulated. If you have need of further blankets, we are well stocked. Please, just remain calm.'

There was an almighty shriek and Jodie came racing out from a door at the far side. Cat recognized the legend on the door, realizing it was the lady's toilet. The girl had obviously been in there for some seven minutes.

'There's no light,' she cried, running up to John. 'There's no light; why are there no lights?'

'It's a power cut.'

'Well, get the lights back on. Denis, get the lights back on.'

'I can't,' said Denis. 'It's not happening within our area; it must be further down. There's nothing I can do; it'll come back on when it comes on. But please, sit down and eat.'

'They'll not come back, they'll not come back if it was a power cut. They'll stay elsewhere. Who's going to sort me out? Who's going to deal with that?'

Catriona stood up, stepped across to the girl, and laid a hand on her arm. 'It's okay,' she said. 'It's just a power cut. Come over here, let's sit and have some drinks, and then afterwards, if the power's not come on, we'll walk you back up.' Jodie allowed Cat to take her over to the bar and sit her down. Cat watched as the woman drank cocktails like they were glasses of tap water.

As the food was served and everyone tried to make the best of the slightly darker atmosphere, John stepped right behind Cat and putting his hands on her shoulders, he whispered in her ear. 'Probably best we just let her keep drinking, knock her out, go to sleep, get her up into her chalet. Something like that. She's quite hysterical when things don't go her way. Right proper diva.'

Catriona gave a nod. She also clocked John's wife, Celia, seeing John with his hands on Cat's shoulders. The woman didn't seem disturbed at all, merely looking over at them before looking away.

Cat reached up with her hand, taking John's off her shoulder and pulling them down close. 'I think that's a good idea. Why don't you sit on the other side of her? We'll keep her locked in between the pair of us.'

John nodded, took the hint, and sat down. In all the excitement, Cat had forgotten about Tiff. Looking over, she saw her sitting by the fire. There was hardly a word out of the girl, but she was engaged with Coralie, clearly talking about skiing of some sort, technique and that. It was almost as if Tiff had found some sort of star, was revelling in her company.

It was three hours later when, accompanied by John Roberts, Catriona dragged Jodie back to her chalet. The girl was practically paralytic. Maybe John's plan was right, but Cat didn't feel the best about this. 'Maybe you should take her into bed,' said John. 'I don't want to be accused of anything. I'll be just outside though if you need any help.'

'Oh, help me throw her on the bed first, then I can sort her,' said Cat.

'The prices we're paying, it's probably a thing Denis and Coralie should be dealing with, but I've got a feeling tonight Denis is going to be up to high dough. He seems to get extremely excited. Unlike Coralie, she's so calm. Lovely girl, lovely girl.'

Cat wondered if the man thought every woman was a lovely girl. It certainly made any compliment coming from John slightly less of a compliment than maybe it should. Once John had stepped out of the room, Cat changed the girl into a pair of silk pyjamas, put the covers over her, and placed her in what she thought approximated to a recovery position. She didn't look like she was going to be sick or anything, but always best to be on the safe side.

I seem to be becoming far too practical, thought Cat. Once she stepped out of the bedroom and found John sitting in the lounge area, she saw him smile. 'Do you want to go back and finish off those cocktails? It's all right; my wife won't be mad. She's probably going to bed soon, anyway, getting ready for tomorrow's skiing.'

'As much as your company is delightful, said Cat, 'I think I need to sort out Tiff. She's not quite a teenager who can look after herself.' It was a polite way of letting the man down and putting a marker in the sand. He nodded and walked Cat back to her own chalet, where Tiff was already inside.

'If you need anything, just let me know,' said John. 'Pop over anytime, absolute delight to meet you.' With that, he was gone.

'Somebody sweet on you?' queried Tiff. 'A bit old for you though.'

Cat shut the door and turned around. 'A bit less of a stage

whisper, please. But if he puts his hands on my shoulders to whisper in my ear again, I think I might have to have a word.'

Chapter 4

The sun was stretching across the sky, beginning to fade, causing Cat to feel a slight chill as she looked around. She remembered the beach well, one of Luigi's estates. Her dead partner had often taken her here. Across from her, Luigi was standing in a pair of tight Speedos holding a rifle in his hands. She watched him shout over his shoulder, 'Pull,' and then his eyes chased the sky before shooting two clay pigeons clean out of the air. Cat looked down in her own hands and saw a rifle.

'Now it's your turn, my little Cat.' She watched him walk round to the back of her and position her shoulders, pointing her weapon up to the air. 'Just watch them and when you're ready, fire away.'

'Pull', came the shout, and Cat's eyes raised to the sky. Quickly she fired two shots and then watched as the clay pigeons sailed on through the air. She remembered this from the last time. She remembered how he joked that she should be president in the Clay Pigeon Protection Society. How he kept going on about they weren't real animals, weren't real birds to shoot, but what she remembered most was that feeling she had now as he began to rub her shoulders. The evening had taken a more fun turn from here, one she remembered well. It all started when she turned around him to hand the rifle back.

But now it was raining. It never rained in Italy at those times. She was now standing in the highlands and you just got a sudden shower up here. There came a cry. Turning quickly, Cat saw Luigi on the ground. He was raving, clutching at his heart, and then he wasn't. He wasn't doing anything. He was just lying there, dead.

Cat shot up in bed. She could feel the sweat. *It's been months now,* she said to herself. *Months and now I start to get these; now I start to dream. Why the hell now?*

Cat heard something move outside her door and then it opened. 'Are you okay?'

'Come on in,' said Cat, realizing her niece was there. She was also confused because her niece rarely showed any sign of concern for her.

'You shouted; you shouted out.'

'What did I shout?'

'Pull, pull, pull,' Tiff said. 'Were you out at some nightclub or something?'

Cat shook her head. She didn't want to tell Tiff about the memory in her head, and she certainly didn't want to tell her how sour it just went. 'Just a nightmare, love. Back to bed, Tiff; you can go for some snowboarding in the morning.'

'I don't know about that; the weather seems quite closed in. Are you sure you're okay? It's not like you to get like this. You don't shout things out. Well, not unless you've had some drinks.'

Cat gave her the stern face. It was something if your mother or father—or maybe even your siblings—have a go at you about what you drank, but you didn't expect it from your niece and not when she did it in that maternal fashion. In the darkness, Cat struggled to see Tiff's face with her long straight hair going down the side of the head. It was just about evident and then it dawned on Cat. There might actually be another reason why she was in here. 'Are you okay?'

'It's kind of cold in the other room. Do you mind if I come in?'

Something must be up, thought Cat. *It's not like Tiff to be like this.* So, she held out her hand and waved her niece over. The beds in the chalet were large, possibly king-size, and Cat thought she could probably hide an orchestra in her bed, never mind her niece. She watched as Tiff made her way around to the side of the bed, threw off her dressing-gown and clambered in under the covers. Cat reached across to put a comforting arm around her.

'Get off. I said it was cold in there. The duvet is fine.'

Cat almost laughed. There was one thing Tiff couldn't take, any sort of close emotion, any physical touch, any sign of normal affection. Part of Cat wondered how Tiff would be if she ever found a man. Or a woman for that matter; who knew these days? That's what her mother had always said, 'Who knew? Who knew that we would get a child like you? Who knew that you would find some sort of Italian?' Her mother's disappointed face came back. *Who cares?* thought Cat, *who cares?* and turned over in the bed. It was a couple of minutes later when she felt Tiff shuffle across and go back to back with her, but that was about it. That was about all the affection you were going to get but it still made Cat smile.

Lying there, Cat could hear the wind. It was through the evening that the clouds had started to set in and now through the night, the wind had built up. Maybe that's what was bothering Tiff rather than the cold, because of the lack of heating. Denis had been true to his word, building a fire inside each chalet, but there was only so much heat that that a fire could produce without being constantly fed. Cat had revelled in the safety of the covers after she'd returned from dropping off Jodie.

Cat couldn't sleep, the dream of Luigi having upset her. At last, she heard Tiff begin to snore. She wondered if she'd ever get back over to sleep herself. Hearing the wind, she remembered a time when she stood outside in Scotland with her beloved partner, facing the weather, as he held her from behind. The memory was a good one, but she wasn't feeling sentimental. It was something else, something more raw that she was missing. Was it his touch? Was it his presence? Something about him being around. When he'd first passed on, she'd been shocked, but now, she was missing all the things about him, more subtle things. The little conceits they passed to each other that no one knew about. In fact, she got annoyed with where he left his toothpaste and the way he used to stare as she would stand in front of the mirror brushing her hair. Just when she'd finished, he'd come along and mess it up again. Cat sniffed, she felt the first trickle of a tear coming from her eyes. 'Damn it,' she said to herself, 'Damn it.'

Something brought Cat outside of herself, a rumbling but not somebody's stomach. And it was loud, very loud. Loud enough to make Cat spring out of bed and grab her dressing gown, wrapping it around her. She made her way quickly to the window and looked out, but all around were the quiet chalets. Each one seemed secure in its area, with nothing much changed except a lack of lights, but the rumbling grew louder and louder still. So much so that she heard her niece turn over in the bed muttering, 'What's that? What on earth's that?'

Indeed, thought Cat, *what on earth's that*? But she wasn't going to wake up her niece to find out. Instead, she decided to remain at the window to see if she could spot what was happening.

One of the doors from the chalet across from her flew open. Cat saw a torchlight moving around. She couldn't tell who it was, but she thought the person had come from Jodie's chalet. Surely, it must be, that's where they dropped her off last night. Cat continued to watch as the figure ran here and there in the snow, and then began to shout. She looked around at the other chalets hoping to see someone come out of them, someone to take charge of the situation, but nothing moved. The light seemed to fall to the ground and then it was up again. It swept about before falling over a second time.

'Heck with this,' said Cat, and made her way out from the bedroom into the hall at the front of the chalet, grabbing her large coat. She pulled her snow boots on, grabbed a torch from a cupboard at the side, and made her way out into the snow. The paths between the chalets had light dustings of snow on them, but it was thick off the path. Hurrying, she made her way across to where the figure now lay in the snow, the torch lying some distance away. As Cat shone her beam towards the person, she saw the face of Jodie.

'It's come, did you hear it? Did you hear it? 'What's happening? We're all going to—We're all going to—'

'Going to what?' said Cat. 'We're not going anywhere; it's okay.'

The girl thrashed about on the ground, pointing this way and that, and the rumbling they'd heard before was still evident. Now she was outside, it was louder still, but Cat thought it was coming from below where the chalets were situated. Much further below.

'Get them to stop it, get them to stop it.'

Cat wasn't sure how to do that; it sounded like it was possibly an avalanche. She had heard one before while skiing with Luigi. It had been some distance off but it sounded like this. Cat was also aware that she was no expert in this field. If it was an avalanche, and it was coming this way, they should get inside. Besides, it was blooming cold out here. She reached down and roughly grabbed the girl's wrist.

'Where are you going? Where are you taking me? What's going on? Do you hear it? Do you hear it?'

'I hear it; now, get up—get inside,' Cat thought she sounded like her mother, which strongly disappointed her. She remembered that strength her mother used to have when she was dealing with Cat as a toddler, pulling her here and there. Instead, Jodie pulled back and Cat tumbled down into the snow.

'What's up with her?'

Cat turned around to see Tiff standing in her dressing gown, no jacket on, and nothing on her feet. 'What are you doing? You'll get cold; go and get something on your feet.'

'I'm fine. You know I don't feel the cold. I'm fine.' It didn't matter what you said to Tiff; once she decided she was doing something, she did it. Rather than try to chastise her again or even convince her, Cat instead wondered what the quickest way was to get Tiff back inside.

'Give me a hand; she needs to go inside.'

'Can you hear it? Can you hear it? You, you,' said Jodie, pointing at Tiff.

'What are you pointing at me for?'

'She's clearly upset,' said Cat. 'Get the other wrist, pull her to her feet with me, and let's get back inside our chalet, please. Come on, Tiff, give me a hand.'

Whether Tiff actually realized the seriousness of the situation, be it an avalanche or just simply becoming frozen on the dark mountainside, she reached down and assisted Cat in pulling Jodie to her feet. Cat put an arm around the woman's waist, though it took a while, and they managed to guide her towards their chalet. Once inside, Cat let Tiff take Jodie through to the main room before she hung up her coat. She searched around before finding some of the emergency candles and lit them, illuminating the lounge area in a vague fashion. It was then she watched as Tiff stood over Jodie, shaking her head.

'She's not making any sense,' said Tiff.

'You heard it, you heard it. Have you got it? Was it you?' and then there was sudden silence and Jodie fell to the floor. Cat watched as the woman began to shake.

'She's cold,' said Tiff. 'Look at her; she's cold.'

Cat stepped forward, not knowing, and put her hand up to Jodie's head where she felt her sweat. 'I'm not sure that's cold.' said Cat, 'More like she's withdrawing from something, like she needs something.' There was a knock at the door. 'Tiff, get that.' said Cat. 'I need to take care of her.'

'Why me?' said Tiff. 'You get it. You said I didn't have any shoes on.'

Cat shook her head. This is another thing about Tiff. She just did what she wanted. If it was something she didn't like, she avoided it, and answering the door to a possible stranger was something she wasn't going to do despite the obvious, more pressing situation in front of her.

'Then kneel down here. In fact, no, get her some blankets, cover her up; just let her lie on the floor but get some blankets.' Cat marched quickly to the front door, opening it to see Denis's face.

'Are you okay? Are you okay? There's been an avalanche further down the mountain. We're cut off. We will be cut off for a while, but are you okay? I heard screaming. I heard screams.'

'That was Jodie, Denis. She's inside but she was running around out there. I don't think she's well. In fact, I think, well, I don't know.'

'What?' asked Denis. 'You think what?'

'She's withdrawing from something. Does she have any medication you know of? Anything they said to you?'

'No, they said very little about her. The entourage, they looked after her.'

'Then where are they?'

'They were giving her, how you say, alone time to straighten herself up. She likes them around to do things, but then she will suddenly get times when she wants to have her own company. Very strange girl. Very strange.'

Catriona saw another figure running out to the chalet, and as it arrived at the steps, she recognized it as the man with the children.

'Are you okay? Julie said she heard screaming, people shouting. Are you okay? I got dressed to see if I could help.'

Cat related the situation to the man and then asked if he'd any experience of medical fashion.

'Well, I am a first responder,' he said.

Thank God for the English accent. It was someone Cat could communicate with well regarding the situation, so she invited the man inside. Cat was aware the man was shaking himself, a little more from nerves than anything else.

'By the way, my name's Gordon. Gordon Plymouth. I'm a musician but I also have first-aid experience so let's get a look at this girl.' Gordon knelt down over Jodie and started opening her eyes and looking. He put his hand on her head as Tiff knelt down beside him, following his every move.

'I think you're right. She does look like she's having some sort of withdrawal, but she seems fit enough with it. Probably best to wrap her up, keep her somewhere warm. If you're up to it, Denis, I think we should check her chalet for any medication just in case that's what she's missing, but I suspect it might be something else.'

'What do you mean, something else?' asked Tiff. 'Do you mean drugs?'

'Yes, I do and—hello, I'm Gordon, how are you?'

'What sort of drugs?' asked Tiff, as if the man had not introduced himself.

'That's Tiffany, my niece,' said Cat. 'I'm Catriona and obviously you've met Denis before.'

'The Contessa.' Cat rolled her eyes. *Not another one.* 'Delighted to meet you. I'm here with Julie, and the kids, Timmy and Howie. I'm a bit of a musician which is one of the ways I know Jodie here, although I think she gets more of the limelight than I ever do. Would you be able to put her into your bed?' asked Gordon. 'Or would you like me to carry her?'

'Probably best you put her in Tiff's bed,' said Cat, and then noticed Tiff's eyes rolling at her. 'Well, you were in mine, or would you rather we have the three of us in that bed in there?' Tiff shook her head and Cat saw Gordon smile at the way the women reacted to each other.

'Show me the way and I'll carry her through. Then I'll go with Denis and find out if her medication is missing.' The man picked up Jodie in his arms as if she were nothing, and Cat led him through to Tiff's bedroom. The duvet was pulled back and Gordon was able to lay Jodie gently on the bed and Cat tucked her in. 'I'll be back in a few minutes,' said Gordon, and marched off with Denis.

'It would have to be my bedroom, wouldn't it?'

'It's okay, Tiff. Look at her, she's not in a good way. We'll wait till the men come back, find out if there's anything else we can give her, then I think we all get back to sleep.'

'Did I hear Denis say avalanche?' asked Tiff.

'Yes, you did. He said there's been an avalanche further down the mountain. It seems we're cut off.'

'Oh, well,' said Tiff. 'It's not going to affect the snow, is it? It's not going to affect me getting out on the board.'

There's been a power cut. There was a woman running around screaming in the night. She was lying down, obviously withdrawing from something, and was now on Tiff's bed. And there was an avalanche. But no, Tiff, thought Cat, as *long as we get out on the snowboard, everything's going to be just okay.*

'I'm sure you'll be fine,' said Cat, smiling at her niece.

Chapter 5

When Gordon had returned with Denis, he reported that a search of the flat had revealed no medication. This confirmed Gordon's suspicion that Jodie was withdrawing from some sort of drug. He had checked the woman's arms looking for needle marks but found none and acknowledged that this meant that she probably sniffed in whatever it was. Denis said that given the money that Jodie was worth, it could be any drug. She certainly could form an expensive habit without noticing it financially.

Catriona had not been up for a large discussion and had politely but firmly sent the gentlemen away once it had been established that Jodie was going to be okay. Shortly after, Cat and Tiff had both returned to the large bed. It took Cat only five minutes to fall asleep. This time, when her mind drifted off into the dreamscape inside it, she was in Scotland, Scotland in the rain with a pair of arms around her that she recognized. This was a dream that would end well. That, she promised herself. She realized that dreams weren't a trip through a set of photographs where you could take out the bad ones, the ones where the camera had misaligned or the focus had gone off, or where there'd been a mess up and you'd accidentally set off the camera. But this one would end well.

Cat woke with a jolt and looked up into the face of Tiff who was shaking her by the shoulders.

'Get up. You need to get up and see. Come, come have a look.'

'Come and have a look at what? It's what? Four in the morning? Tiff, get back into bed.'

'No, you have to come and see this.'

'See what?'

'Come and see this. Come.' Tiff left the room and Cat swung herself out of the bed for her feet to find their slippers, before grabbing her dressing gown. She plunged into the main lounge area before hearing Tiff call from her own bedroom. Shaking her hair out as she walked and realizing that it was still a little knotted, Cat made her way into the other bedroom where only an hour or two ago she had laid the singer on the bed. As she walked in, she noticed that the covers were thrown back and the bed was now empty.

'Where the hell has she gone?'

'That's why I wanted you to come and see.'

'Did you hear her leave?' said Cat.

'No, but she's not here.'

'So why were you up?'

'Because I needed a drink and then I came in to see if she was okay. I had a look at her.'

'You just wanted to see what was happening. That's why you were in. You were nosing, weren't you?'

'No,' said Tiff. 'I was just checking up on things and then she's not here.'

Cat wanted to pursue her line of enquiry and to make Tiff admit that she was having a nosy, but there were clearly more important issues here. 'No, she's not here, is she?' said Cat and made her way back into the lounge area hunting for and then finding the paging device Denis had given them on their arrival. She pressed it before entering her bedroom and quickly changing her clothes. Denis was quick, maybe three minutes at most. Cat had her jeans and jumper on when she answered the door.

'What's the matter?' said a very weary Denis.

'Jodie is gone, Denis. I don't know when and I don't know where. Given the state she was in, I think we need to go and find her.'

'Yes. Yes, we need to. We need to. Oh God, no. What's happening? What's happening? No. No.'

Cat took hold of Denis by the shoulders. 'Calm down. Go get Gordon. Go and get Gordon.' Denis looked up into Cat's eyes and for a moment she thought he might've seen clarity before he started shaking again, going back into that panic. 'Just get Gordon,' said Cat. Denis bolted off.

'Why are you getting Gordon?' asked Tiff.

'Because we need to go and search for this woman. Look at Denis. He's as panicked as anything. You saw Gordon earlier. He was very rational.'

'It's not that, is it? I think you like Gordon. I could tell, you had that slight smile that you do and you flicked your hair.'

Cat was ready to fight back but Tiff was right. She had been impressed with him, but he was a married man. 'Okay. So yes, he is quite impressive. Isn't he? But he's also very confident, and that's what we need now. Go and get changed. He can help us.'

'I'm not going out of there. It's cold. I need to sleep. I'm tired.'

'What do you mean you're too tired? Tiff, we've got someone

out there in the cold withdrawing from drugs, probably. She could end up dead.'

'It's okay. You've got Gordon,' said Tiff, turning around and walking back to the bedroom. 'Gordon will help you find her. Don't worry. I'm off to bed.' With that, Tiff disappeared into the bedroom, closing the door. Cat felt a rage grow inside her that Tiff should come to help, but then she thought it was maybe for the best. She wouldn't have to worry about her niece—she'd be happily sleeping. Cat would go and help Gordon. It was another four or five minutes before Denis appeared back at the door with Gordon and a red-haired woman.

'This is Contessa Monroe, Catriona,' said Gordon to the woman beside him. 'And this Cat, is Julie.'

'Just call me Red,' said the woman. Cat could see why. Her hair was a deep ruby, not some sort of strawberry blonde. She had the appearance of an athletic woman, plenty of muscle, looking in remarkably good shape for someone who had had two kids.

'I'm all geared up' said Cat. 'What do we do? How do we go about this?' At first, everyone looked towards Denis, but it was obvious he was in a panic.

'I thought you would have a plan, Gordon. Maybe you would know what to do'. Cat saw Gordon look, first of all, towards Julie and she gave a nod and the man began to speak.

'Let's check the other chalets first. She may have wandered into one of them. The others could be holding her, looking after her. Then after that, I think we start to fan out, there are a couple of observation huts in the vicinity where the bird watchers go. You know John Roberts? Cat, you go and find him. I'll go to the students. Red, you go and see if Bertrand's in. Denis, go and get Coralie. She can help us search as well.'

'What about your kids?' asked Cat.

'The kids will be fine,' said Julie. 'They're fast asleep. They won't leave. I have left them a note on the inside of the door.'

Cat wasn't sure if this was the best plan, but she'd never been a mother and there were plenty other things to get on with. With her coat wrapped up around her and a bobble hat on and her hair in a ponytail behind her, Catriona made her way over to the Roberts's chalet. She banged loudly on the door. Once she got no response, Cat went round to the windows and started banging on them. It took a few minutes before she heard the front door open. Cat raced back towards it.

'What is it?' said Sylvia Roberts, appearing at the door. Cat looked up at the tall woman with well-built shoulders and short black hair. 'I'm sorry to bother you', said Cat, 'but Jodi's gone missing.'

'That diva, that girl with her group of people that keep on making all the noise? Frankly, go and get them to go and look for her.'

'They're not back. They're not here and they're not coming,' said Cat. 'An avalanche has cut us off, but she's missing and she's withdrawing from something. Drugs or something. I think her life's at risk.'

'Well, why don't you go and get Denis?' said Celia.

'I have done. I've also got Gordon and Julie and they're getting everyone else together, hopefully to go and look for her. Can you help? Can you grab John as well?'

'John's not here. He likes to photograph birds and animals. He says night time is one of the best times for wildlife. He's probably out in one of the huts already.'

Cat looked around in the dark. It was cold and there was

little light, other than the torches she saw running around the compound at this time. *Who goes out at this time to watch wildlife?* She felt a shudder go down her back. Not something Cat would be doing.

'Okay, well, can you come yourself?' She watched Celia nod, and the woman disappeared back inside for a few moments before returning fully kitted up in a jacket and thermal trousers, snow boots on her feet, and additional bobble hat and a torch hanging at her side. Celia was ready and the two women walked back towards Cat's chalet where she saw a line of torches.

'Have you rounded everyone up, Gordon?', asked Cat.

'It's a pretty mixed bag. Some of the students are missing. Quite frankly, some of the others are too far gone to be of any use. We don't want to be losing anybody else out here. It appears Bertrand's not in.'

'I have these maps. They're very basic, but they will show you where hides are.'

This was a new voice. As a torch was moved up towards the woman's face, Cat saw Coralie. She was maybe in her forties and unlike Denis, appeared incredibly calm.

'It's cold, so I say we go in pairs and don't go too far. It'll be daylight in another two to three hours then we can search more properly but until then, stay close to the compound. Don't go further than these hides here.' Coralie pointed to a number of marks on the map.

'Good plan, Coralie,' said Gordon. 'I suggest that I head off with Julie. Coralie, you take Catriona, and Celia, if you head off with Denis, that'll give us three parties to search. Catriona and Coralie search over here on the west side. I'll take the east, and you take north of us, Denis. No more than an hour of searching and then come back here and report. Remember, if you get too cold or things not going well, just come back. We don't want to lose anybody else out there.'

Cat looked around at the little team and although she felt slightly disappointed that she wasn't going with Gordon, she was glad that she wasn't stuck with Denis. Coralie didn't wait for her and struck out towards the west with Cat tailing in her wake. Snow was thick underfoot and Cat found herself having to drag her feet through it. Coralie, despite being the older woman between them, was clearly the fitter. She almost moved through the snow as if it was not there.

'Are you okay? Sorry, I'm striking out in front because I know this place. If I get too far ahead, shout me back, yes? Call to me.'

'Of course. I can see why Tiff was impressed with you. She's dead keen for you to take her out on the snowboard.'

'Well, let's hope we find Jodi and don't have to go searching tomorrow,' said Coralie. 'There are a couple of hides out here and even if she's in her shivery state, she might seek shelter at some point so I think we should check them.' The pair disappeared into a wood where the snow became less thick underfoot, and Cat found it easier to walk. As she trundled along, light sweeping this way and that in the darkness, she picked up the freshness of the trees. There was a stillness in the air, a calmness with only the wind blowing through the trees above. It had been howling earlier on in the night. Now, while there was still a breeze to the air, here in the shelter of the forest, it felt much calmer. Maybe she had instinctively gone for shelter here.

Jodie hadn't been wearing much, and she would become cold quickly. Despite the tiredness she felt, Cat plodded on as best she could. Coralie had routed them past two shelters, which both turned out to be empty. They had little peepholes in them, somewhere to stick a camera through. Coralie explained they were hides, as the wildlife around here could be quite spectacular, if you like that sort of thing. They had been walking for some three-quarters of an hour, but Coralie explained there were more hides to check before turning back and routing through the forest again by a different route. Sweeping the torches through the trees, Cat suddenly felt tired and saw Coralie in the distance ahead.

After a while, the instructor turned around, shouting back to Cat, 'Are you okay? It's just here. The hide is just here. I will wait here in the hide for you. Catch up.'

'Fine,' said Cat. 'Not a problem. I'm just catching my breath.' Cat leaned forward, hands on her knees, breathing in the cool air. She was starting to feel a little cold, nothing dangerous, but she'd be glad to be heading back soon. On her face, there was sweat from the exertion and she wondered how parts of her body were sweating underneath the coat, and yet inside, her bones almost felt a singular chill. When she got back, she'd pop in to the jacuzzi or the shower. *Oh, no,* she thought, p*ower cut. We'll have to heat water up in the fire. Maybe we'll stay smelly for a day or two.*

As these thoughts were racing through Cat's head, she casually swept her torch to one side and saw a figure in the snow. Making her way towards it, Cat heard a cry from up ahead.

'I found her,' said Coralie. 'Jodie's in the shelter. I found her. Come up to me and we'll get her back.'

Cat stopped in her tracks. She'd just seen a figure herself. *It was a figure, wasn't it?* The torch had just glanced past it. Cat held her torch up and moved the beam across the previous spot. This time, she found a couple of skis sticking upright in the snow. Sweeping the beam further around, she could find nothing to the right, but she swept the beam back to the left and it shone upon a leg in the snow.

'Coralie, there's somebody else out here.'

'What?' Coralie cried from up ahead. 'I've got Jodie. Let's head back.'

'We can't. There's someone else here.' Cat made her way to the figure, the beam sweeping down. The person must have been at least six-foot, but the hair, the hair seemed long. This wasn't a man's figure. Cat knelt down beside it, her heart beginning to tremble.

'Hello. Are you okay? Hello.' She put her hand out and shook the body, but there was no response. She reached down, grabbed the shoulder, and pulled as hard as she could, rolling the figure over, but the arm seemed locked and she struggled to complete the manoeuvre. The figure got halfway over, and Cat held it there, taking her torch and placing it right in front of the body's face.

Eyes looked back at her, eyes that were cold with no life. It was the woman she had seen arguing with her boyfriend, one of the students. Alice. It was Alice.

Chapter 6

The fire in the main building was blazing after Coralie had piled more logs on it. In fact, Cat could feel the heat on her back. Although she felt physically better, warmer, there was something inside running very cold. After the incident on the cruise ship, one where Tiff had recovered a dead body, she had hoped this would be a proper holiday, a time away, but it seemed it was not to be. After finding the body, Cat had remained there, but Coralie had returned Jodie back to the main compound and then brought others out to assist with taking Alice's body back. Cat wondered if this had been wise. Maybe it should've been left in situ for the authorities to work with it, but Coralie had been quite insistent. She deemed it to be an offense to leave a body like that. What if someone else came upon it? Clearly there had been an accident.

But Coralie said to Cat that she was not sure how it had occurred. The skis were stuck up in the snow some distance behind the body which had been thrown forward. But what had Alice been doing out skiing at that time of night? Cat thought about the others who were also missing. Bertrand Jobert had been out of his chalet, as had John Roberts. The students were struggling to remember who was in and who was out. That was at least seven people, and Jodie was also out and about, although, quite high. She couldn't have caused any incident in her state . . . could she? Cat didn't know.

Denis had assumed it was an accident right from the off, but Gordan Plymouth had been asking some difficult questions. The position of the body after coming off of the skis was wrong for somebody to have been pitched that far forward. And what had caused her to tumble? How'd she been going at such a speed with no ski poles? Of course, Denis had phoned through to the police, but with the cloud cover over the mountain and the avalanche on the road, the compound was cut off. Although there was no electricity, they were okay for food and had heat generated by the fires. Without this incident, they would've been fine. Just a case of waiting it out until things got better. Maybe the power would be coming back on soon, although they reckoned it could take a couple of days to clear the avalanche from the road below. That, of course, was depending on how bad they found it to be once they started to clear the snow. Plus, the weather conditions were poor further down the mountain. Here in the higher reaches, although the wind was not strong, there was a lot of cloud cover and hence no helicopter could get through.

Denis had insisted that everyone come back and sit in the main building so he could speak to everyone. Some were there in coats, but clearly had their pyjamas on underneath. The only people missing were the two children. Coralie, after she had brought the body back to the main chalet, had made some food and hot soup was passed around. Cat was unsure what Denis was actually doing, but he did seem to be in a flap and constantly on and off the phone. After a period, he seemed to collect himself and stand before everyone, flapping his hands for attention, despite the fact that everyone had gone quiet at his arrival.

'I am sorry to wake you up at this time of night, but there has been a tragic accident. Alice Tarney, I'm afraid, has died. She broke her neck while skiing in the dark.' The sobs of Kyle Cobbler could be heard in the background, and Cat saw Sara Lyons rubbing her hand on his shoulder. 'I'm afraid we still have to store Alice in one of our side rooms here, as the emergency services cannot get through. As you know, we have a power cut, but there was also an avalanche tonight, further down the mountain that's caused the road to be blocked. And with the cloud cover expected to stay for a few days, we can't fly out. So here we have it. I intend that we stay, and I will be available, as will Coralie, to feed you, to keep the fires going, but I ask that you don't do any strenuous activity. We can't deal with any further casualties. And may I extend my condolences to yourself, Mr. Cobbler, and to the rest of your group. Please look after each other.'

With that, he stopped abruptly, leaving Cat feeling that something else should've been said. She glanced over at Gordon Plymouth, who glanced back, shrugging his shoulders. Cat stepped forward, addressing the group.

'Denis is right; we've all had a bit of a shock, so I think we should all head back and get what sleep we can before morning. Although it's practically here. Let's have a morning in bed relaxing and trying to recuperate.'

'I'm not going anywhere on my own,' said Jodie. 'I'm not. Not after something like that.'

'Calm down, Jodie,' said Cat. 'You can come to ours. That's not a problem, and I suggest everyone else goes back to their chalets.' In the corner, Bertrand Jobert stood up, still dressed in his black with dark glasses on, despite the time at night.

'You won't find me in my chalet. I came here to spend time in the hides. I will be out in the hides. I can buzz Denis if I need anything today.' With that, Bertrand strolled out, and the group turned to watch him march across the snow, heading first to his chalet, and then a moment later departing with a larger coat and a backpack over his shoulder.

'That's, of course, his choice,' said Cat, 'but the rest of us, I suggest, like myself, go to our chalets, and if you're feeling unsafe, lock your door.'

It was strange, but the group almost looked at Cat for direction. Something that the Contessa tag bestowed upon her in a thoroughly undeserved fashion. Maybe she tried to step up to the mark, but really, she was ill-prepared for it. As soon as she'd finished speaking and went to sit down again, Tiff grabbed her.

'Does that mean that I don't get to go on the half pipe? Do you think Coralie will have time?'

'Tiff, somebody's just died. Let's get to the chalet and spend the morning getting some sleep.'

'I did get sleep. I was asleep when you went off looking around the place for Jodie.'

'Tiff, I need your help right now. Can you get that?' Cat held her niece by the shoulders, gazing into her eyes, looking for some sort of recognition. But Tiff turned away and strode off towards the chalet. Sometimes she couldn't see it, could she? Whatever it was that went on in Tiff's head was what Tiff saw. Not what anybody else required. It no longer made Cat angry; it was just frustrating, but that's the way Tiff was. There was plenty else about her that made up for it.

Gordon Plymouth came over with Julie and asked if he could

assist getting Jodie back up to the chalet. The singer put her hand up, indicating no help was required. Cat looked at the woman's face. Her eyes were sullen and sunken, but she did look better than when they found her.

'I think what Jodie needs is a bit of rest, and maybe a little TLC. Thanks, Gordon. I'll get her back. I suggest you and Julie get back to your kids.'

'Julie's kids,' said Gordon. 'I'm the uncle. It's Julie's kids.'

'Oh, right.' said Cat, 'I didn't realize.' But something inside her jumped. Why do these things always happen at the wrong time? Just accept him for the nice man that he is. 'Well, thanks for your help, Gordon. I'll see you later, and thank you, Julie.'

'I can't believe you're actually a Contessa,' said Julie. 'You must talk to me about that sometime. What it's like being royalty?' Inside, Cat rolled her eyes, but she smiled pleasantly and nodded, allowing the woman to depart before making her way to Jodie. Before she could reach her, Cat was intercepted by Denis.

'Make sure she's okay. Make sure nothing happens to her. It's particularly important. It's my job on the line if something happens to her. God knows the job's not good as it is, but Alice was just a student. They won't care the same. Jodie's a superstar, the press will be everywhere if something happens to her. Make sure you look after her, Contessa.'

Contessa now? thought Cat. *Everybody uses the Contessa word when they want something from me. It's almost like some sort of status that you had to live up to, that you had to suddenly become something. Sometimes, I know how the queen feels.*

'Don't worry, Denis. I will look after her. She seems to be mobile now anyway, so let's get to bed, you too. I think you need as much sleep as the rest of us.'

'I have reports to fill. I have things to do.'

Cat put her hand onto Denis's shoulder. 'Look, we're stuck up here. Where's your report going to go?'

'Well, we have the internet,' said Denis.

'We do,' said Cat, 'but they don't know that. Switch it off. Just don't send anything for an hour or two. Get yourself some sleep. Stuff them. Alice is dead. As much as I regret that, she's dead. We can't help her. We can help you. Get some sleep.'

Cat was impressed by the way she was taking charge of this and Coralie, over Denis's shoulder, was giving an approving nod of the head. 'Such a terrible accident though,' said Denis.

From over his shoulder, Coralie frowned. 'That's never an accident. How? How did those skis get there? It's not right, Denis. It's not right. We need to keep our eyes open.'

Cat saw Denis shake. He clearly was a man not geared up for this. 'No, no,' said Denis, 'it's an accident. Just an accident. That's all we have. And now we sleep. The Contessa is right; we sleep so we don't get the press. Thank goodness for the avalanche. There's no press, but please, you take care of her, and Coralie, stop it. Stop telling me we have somebody here who's killed. This is an accident. A sad but tragic accident. It has to be.' With that, Denis strolled off, leaving Cat looking at Coralie.

'You don't believe it's an accident, do you?' asked Coralie.

'In truth, I don't see how it is, but I have my hands full. I can't go running around investigating at the moment.' And something else bothered Cat that she didn't say. Tiff hadn't mentioned anything. Of all the people around any investigations who would stick their nose in, Cat was expecting Tiff to do it. But she was worried she would set Denis off.

'If somebody did kill her, Coralie, then I don't know who.

We don't know anybody here or if there was trouble amongst the group of students. That would seem the likely place, but why? They all seemed to get on well. Now Alice and Kyle had been rowing all the time, but you see him today. He's a mess.'

'Just because you killed someone doesn't mean you can't grieve for them,' said Coralie, coldly. The idea hadn't entered Cat's head, and she felt a bit stunned by how quickly the woman had suggested it.

'I suppose that's true, but we've no evidence, so I think it's time we headed for bed.' With that, Cat walked over to Jodie who was sitting by the fire, shoulders slumped, head down.

'Are you okay?'

'No. I need water.'

'But you've stopped shaking.'

'Yes, it's sorted.'

Cat wasn't sure by what she meant by sorted, but clearly, she wasn't in a great mood to be asked anything. So, Cat took her arm gently, indicating she should rise and head back up to the chalet. It took a while because Jodie walked slowly and was wrapped up in a blanket to make the journey to the chalet. She'd been out without her coat, out in that cold in a hide, but thankfully the fire revived her. Previously in Cat's chalet, the woman had shivered even though it wasn't cold. Shivering from whatever withdrawal she was having, but now she walked as if nothing was really wrong except a general malaise or tiredness.

'You can have Tiff's room, but please, don't disappear off again. I don't want to go running around looking for you. It was damn cold. You put the rest of us at risk when you do that.'

Jodie stopped on the step to the chalet and turned to Cat.

'I don't know who you think you are. They all look at you because you're a Contessa. I'm the star here. If I want to run off, I'll go off.'

'You can do that,' said Cat, 'but I'm not damn well coming after you. Next time you can freeze to death.' Catriona was astounded by the harshness of her tongue, but she also couldn't believe the brazen selfishness of this girl. For someone who looked beautiful on the outside, she certainly was as horrible in the interior as you could get. She let Jodie walk into the chalet before turning around on the step and saw the daylight slowly breaking through. The cloud cover was still solid, but it was brighter. As she went to turn back into her chalet, she saw Gordon making his way up to his own and he stopped, giving her a wave. Cat waved back, a sudden warmness flowing through her, but then she turned away, stepping inside the chalet. There was no time for that at the moment, even if Catriona did feel a little better about Julie being his sister. Cat wasn't sure where her feelings were going, especially the dreams she'd been having about Luigi so she decided to just let everything slide, get on with the job in hand, get some sleep, and then get some people up here to sort this place out. She'd have to make sure it was done. Coralie looked useful, but she was hell bent on causing an incident, looking for murder.

Jodie disappeared into Tiff's room, slamming the door shut and causing Tiff to rise from Cat's room. 'So, can I go in the half-pipe tomorrow? Or today?'

'Whatever,' said Cat, 'but, if you break a leg we can't get anybody here; that's what Denis said.'

'Yeah, I heard him, I won't. I'm good at it, you know that. I'm good on the snowboard.'

'You are,' said Cat. 'You are good but accidents happen.'

'It didn't happen here though, did it? From what you said, from what I heard, that wasn't an accident out there. Do you need me to help?'

Cat stood almost in disbelief. 'Do I need you to help? Help with what?'

'Your investigation. You were taking charge down there, I assume you're going to investigate this, find out what happened. Denis isn't going to, he's rubbish. You've seen him, he's shaking like a leaf. Maybe I should help. After all, I'm the one who sorted that last time.' Cat stood with her hands on her hips before taking off her coat, hanging it up, and kicking off her snowshoes. She made her way to the bedroom, got undressed, and clambered into bed, hearing Tiff climb in on the other side.

'I am happy to help, obviously, I want to get some snowboarding in, but I am happy to help.'

Catriona shook her head. *Let's just get out of here,* she thought, *and anyway, I need to sleep. Time to say hello to Luigi again.*

Chapter 7

'Luigi, get the door.'

'Luigi's not here. Why'd you think Luigi was here?'

Cat shot bolt upright in bed, turned her head this way and that. Tiff was standing on the edge of the bed, fully dressed in her snowboarding outfit.

'There was a knock at the door,' said Cat. 'I was lying with Luigi, his hand on my back. It was breakfast. Breakfast was coming. I'm sure it was breakfast. He would go and get it; he'd bring it in on the table, the trolley thing. He would open it up and we'd have it. Kippers, Tiff. Kippers. We had kippers that time.'

'Well, you're not there. He's not here. We're in our chalet and breakfast would've been some time ago. It's now after lunch.'

'After lunch?' said Cat. 'Why didn't you get me up?'

'Because you were tired—you were sleeping. Why would I get you up? I went snowboarding.'

Cat looked at her niece and then began to smile. 'Was it good?'

'Yes,' said Tiff. 'And then to help you with your investigation, I went out looking at where that girl died last night. I saw the skis and I think I saw where the body was. That wasn't an accident.'

'Keep that to yourself,' said Cat. 'And we'd better answer the door.'

As if on cue, the door was rapped loudly again. A shout from the other bedroom demanded that the door be answered.

'I see our guest continuing her run of being the most demanding woman in the universe,' said Cat.

'She is right though,' said Tiff; 'that door needs answering.'

'And I'm lying here in my nightwear and you're dressed in a snowsuit. Do you think you could go and get the door, Tiff?' said Cat.

'I need a shower and to get changed.'

'What shower? It's not working. If you're lucky, you might get a bath if you can get some water over the fire. Make yourself something that way.'

'That's a good idea,' said Tiff, and disappeared off.

'Front door. Answer the door,' said Cat.

'Who's being a diva now?' said Tiff, and completely ignored the front door. Cat hauled herself out of bed, pulled her dressing gown around her, ran her hand through her hair more to just confirm how bad it was, as opposed to trying to fix it, and then opened the chalet's front door in a rush. There, standing in a large jacket and bobble hat, was Gordon.

'Hi, I was just popping around everyone to see if anyone needed any assistance, see if you're okay. You didn't make it down for any lunch. Denis had cooked, so I thought maybe we should bring something up to you. Are you okay?'

'I'm fine,' said Cat, 'just fine.' And then her hand shot up to her hair again. *But my hair's a mess. I'm stood in my nightwear. I probably stink from being in the bed, and you turn up like this. You could've given me warning. I could've got up. I could've got prepared. I could've looked good.* But of course, Gordon heard none of this. Cat's inner voice continued to berate her as she smiled at the man and said, 'How thoughtful. You need to forgive me, Gordon, but the shower's not working. I've only just got up. Maybe I can get myself together and head down and get some food.'

'How's Jodie?' he asked. 'Do you think she'll want to come down with us?'

In her mind, Cat said, *No, no, she won't. No, she won't.* But to Gordon she said, 'I'll take a look and see.' Turning away, Cat walked to Tiff's bedroom, looked inside, where Jodie appeared to be asleep. She couldn't have been that asleep because she had cried out just a few moments ago to get the door, but no, she was asleep. Best not to disturb. Cat would get changed and Gordon could take her down for something to eat.

Cat returned to the door and asked Gordon if he wanted to come in while she got changed. The man thanked her politely, stepped inside, and stood in the lounge while Cat disappeared into the bedroom. She tried to be quick, but ultimately her hair needed to be brushed. Once she was dressed, she began to stand in front of the mirror to brush her hair, but realized that the time she was taking meant the guy must be standing there looking around wondering what this insane woman was doing. So, she opened the door, entered the lounge beaming as best she could at him.

'Sorry, just getting the hair done.'

'Oh, Julie's the same, or Red as we call her at home. She's got some streak of hair, hasn't she? Like yourself. It's quite curly though, isn't it?'

'It is,' said Cat, brushing her hair down. 'It can take a while to get a hold of, but hey, shall we go down to eat? Otherwise you're going to be standing here forever.'

'I don't mind,' said Gordon, although Cat thought he clearly did. No man wants to stand there and watch a woman brushing her hair, well at least not any man who was normal. You did hear about those other sorts of guys. *No, Luigi wasn't one of them*, thought Cat, and disappeared back into the bedroom. She grabbed a hair tie, and having quickly fixed her hair into a shape that meant it wouldn't flop around or get in the way, she emerged and grabbed a bobble hat, hiding it instantly. *I'm really quite vain.*

As they made their way down to the main building, Cat saw Denis at the chalet of the students. He seemed to be getting an earful from Debbie, the girl with the rich father. No doubt it was fraught within that chalet, having lost their friend, and who knew how Kyle must be feeling, now his girlfriend was dead?

'How's it been this morning?' said Cat, 'I assume you didn't sleep much. You have that manner. Wanting to make sure everything's okay, looking after everyone.'

'I wouldn't say that, but the kids were up and I thought Julie should get some sleep. She's done remarkably well as a single mum raising the pair of them. I do my best to help, but we don't live close enough. I thought bringing her out here was one of the best things to do. She's got an interesting past.'

'Oh,' said Cat, 'in what way?'

'In the way that you can't tell,' said Gordon. 'A woman of many talents, my sister.'

Well, that kind of closes that line of conversation, thought Cat. 'How's the rest of it been here, though? Denis looks like he's getting an earful over there.'

'Oh, God bless the man. He's trying to sort things out, but

he's really quite useless. I think he's quite shocked by what's gone on. I mean, we're all shocked, but he's not handling it. His assistant's much better, Coralie. She organized all the food, got everybody going. She's made sure we got enough, not just to survive, but at least to be fairly comfortable. I mean, the chalet's warm enough; the fire's been blazing in ours. We've all the doors open. It's not a problem at all. I had the kids this morning making snowmen. Didn't really want them to know. They'll not miss Alice, anyway. Best not to get them worried.'

'Indeed not,' said Cat, 'but if you need somebody to help look after them, give me a shout. I'll come with you.'

Cat saw the smile on the man and guessed he saw it for what it was. Catriona did not like kids. They got in the way. Tiff was hard enough to deal with, never mind having a pair of younger ones, charging around, not listening to you, wanting to climb all over you, eating their bogeys or whatever else they did. It might be worth it for getting an extra hour with this man. But there was something inside Cat, something that told her to beware. We had another body. He was a nice man. In fairness, he wasn't trying to be all over her, but last time, that sleaze bag on the boat had taken her for a ride. She'd need to be more careful this time. But she thought Gordon might be more of a gentleman. Down in the main building, Gordon popped through to the kitchen and cooked Cat some bacon on a roll. It wasn't fancy. In fact, it was fairly plain. Cat wondered if she could actually make better herself, but along with a large cup of coffee, it started to revive her. What was picking her up much more was the man opposite in this conversation.

'You really took charge last night, didn't you? You've got that about you, that ability.'

'Ability? Never,' said Cat. 'I've got a name, Contessa.

Everybody acts like you're somebody, the queen or something. It really means so little. Luigi just had land. He had titles, you know? He was a normal person. He was fun, a lot of fun.'

'How long has it been?'

'A few months,' said Cat. 'A few months. Yes. I think I'm starting to really miss certain things now.'

'It can't be easy,' said Gordon, smiling.

'You never married yourself?' asked Cat.

'Never. I had a few relationships. Never went anywhere. I don't think I was ever good enough in the end for them. You try your best, don't you, but some women just—well, I shouldn't say this to a woman like yourself, some women are just so demanding.' Cat smiled. If this would've come from the lips of any other man, she might have rounded on him and told him to stop being so sexist, but from Gordon, it just seemed like a heartfelt thing, something he had experienced. Maybe he had been unlucky, or maybe Cat was just being overgenerous because she liked the look of him.

'What do you think about the accident?' asked Cat.

'It wasn't an accident,' said Gordon, suddenly becoming serious. 'My sister said it was definitely not an accident. Really bizarre. Skis stuck there as if she crashed and fell off them. Skis don't go sticking upright like that. That's almost comical. It's like something you'd see in a cartoon. And there are no ski poles either. What? She just shuffled out? She wasn't on a slope, she was in the forest. If you're going to navigate your way amongst those trees, you'd have ski poles to push yourself.'

'That's what I was thinking,' said Cat, beaming at the man, 'but if that's the case—'

'It means that somebody here is a killer. It means our decision to leave the kids on their own, locked in the chalet last night, was not a good one. I fear that one of us is going to be hanging around the kids a lot more. Normally, I would've let them go out and play in the snow in front of the chalet this morning on their own, caught some sleep, told them to come back in . . . but not with a possible killer on the loose.'

Gordon was keeping his voice low, and Cat watched his eyes as she saw several of the students entering the main building.

'Morning,' shouted Gordon. 'Anything we can help you with?'

Debbie, the girl whose father was paying for their trip, shook her head. 'I think we all just need a bit of space,' said Debbie. 'Denis has been all over us. Just need a bit of peace and quiet to deal with this.'

'Hear you loud and clear,' shouted Gordon. 'We'll keep our kids away from you.'

Cat watched the girl and the others following as they made their way to the bar. Soon they seemed to be pouring whiskeys all round, and despite a mild urge to join them, Cat restrained herself, sitting at a small table with Gordon, her eyes staring at them.

'Don't watch them too closely like that. You'll burn a hole in their back,' laughed Gordon.

'It's probably one of them though, isn't it? I mean, nobody else knows anyone up here. The rest of us are strangers to each other.'

'That's a mighty big assumption,' said Gordon.

'I feel that somebody needs to get to know them,' said Cat.

'They're a bit young for me,' said Gordon, 'A long time since I was student, ten, fifteen years.'

What age was this guy? thought Cat. She had put him late twenties, but the way he was talking was more like mid-thirties, maybe up. Did that matter?

If it had been a murder, somebody needed to get on this. Tiff said she would help, but she wasn't going to be able to get close to people. She wasn't going to be able to find out who people were. She could look at the technical side and she'd work out how it was done, what it was done with. That was what Tiff was good at, but Cat, Cat needed to get in amongst the people. She needed to understand who the people were. Who knew whom? Who was upset with whom?

'You're right, Gordon. We do need to get to know them, and I'm the one who could get close. Thank you for walking me down. Trust me when I say I'd rather stay here and talk to you, but I think I need to go and start finding some things out. I'll see you later.' Cat stood up and Gordon put out his hand, stopping her momentarily.

'Just promise me one thing,' he said in a whisper, 'Be very careful. If one of them's a killer, you'll be at risk, too.'

Cat reached down and took his hand. 'That's very touching, but I'll watch my back, and I'll see you later.' With that, she let her hand slip off from him but kept her eyes on his until she'd taken a few steps away. Walking over to the students, she made an approach straight to Debbie as the girl dropped a whiskey down her throat. So, it was going to be like that, was it?

'Any of you guys know how to make a good cocktail?'

Chapter 8

Tiff had enjoyed her morning, although she hadn't got to use the halfpipe in the way that she wanted. She had managed to board for at least an hour, coming down through some slopes with Coralie. The woman had been busy because these other people in the resort seemed to want her twenty-four/seven to make up this and that, and then there'd been the bother of the dead woman and paperwork. Coralie had been up most of the night, but she enjoyed her ride with Tiff, or at least Tiff thought so.

Tiff had impressed with some of her turns and kicks, and she'd certainly outgunned Coralie down some of the slope. Maybe it had been good for the woman to have got away for a bit, to be able to throw responsibilities to the wind. Responsibilities weren't good. Tiff had seen Cat too often weighed down by them. Her aunt would be better following Tiff's example. For instance, running over and finding out that dead body. Tiff had been tired and she'd gone to sleep, and then in the morning, she'd been fresh, unlike her aunt.

Anyway, she obviously had a thing for that Gordon man. Having seen her aunt, first of all, follow Gordon for something to eat, and then to suddenly to get in with a bunch of students, which seemed to involve simply drinking, Tiff decided she needed a bit more entertainment and went to see Coralie. The poor girl looked under pressure. When she asked Tiff if she would help carry supplies out to the chalets, Tiff agreed. She was nothing if not helpful, Tiff—certainly in her own mind. Mostly, it was fetching and carrying of logs and Tiff had spent a while pushing a wheelbarrow back and forward, dropping logs at the front door of the chalets.

Coralie had said not to go in, especially with everyone having jitters after the death of Alice. Tiff saw no reason why anyone should fear her; after all, Tiff hadn't been awake. Tiff had been in bed and she was the investigator, not the criminal. Surely people could see that, but it was hard to investigate when her aunt was running off, drinking with everyone else. She paid back her friend who had taken her boarding earlier on and once the log supplies had been complete, Tiff ran back and forward with some fresh linen. Coralie was busy cooking and with other duties, and she seemed greatly pleased with Tiff and promised her that the next day she'd take her on the half-pipe properly.

Denis kept watching Tiff though, every time she took supplies. The man seemed nervous as anything. He obviously didn't know her detective skills and what she could do and saw her as a possible killer. Then again, Denis didn't say anything about the killer; he kept reiterating how much of an accident it had been. Maybe he had caused it, maybe that was it, some sort of clever endeavour. It seemed unlikely though; the man didn't seem to have the stomach for it.

Tiff came down for her last run, which involved taking some bottles to drop at Bertrand's. Obviously, the man drank alone because she never saw him down in the bar. As she set the bottles down, he approached the door, opened it, and soon dragged the bottles inside. There was no thank you and Tiff found this extremely rude, so she stood there until the man emerged again. This time, however, he was dressed in black, sunglasses on, hat on his head, and disappeared off with his lens and other photographic gear in a backpack over his shoulder. Tiff was not happy with this; after all, where was the man going? He had been out the night before, and he had not been around whenever Alice died, according to Cat. He had said that he went to the hides to look at animals—to bird watch was the rumour—but the other day, he'd been watching someone.

Tiff had no further jobs to do for Coralie and coming to a loose end, she couldn't really go skiing again. Coralie made it clear that it was better if she did it tomorrow with the instructor. Tiff decided that she would try to follow Bertrand and saw the man leaving the compound and stepping out into the woods.

Tiff was already dressed in her snow boots and jacket, having carried the supplies up, so she simply followed him, trying to keep her distance as he cut in and passed by this tree and that. Although it was daylight, there was a large amount of cloud cover, so amongst the trees, it was reasonably gloomy. Tiff proceeded through the snow until she saw Bertrand disappear inside a hide. Finding a spot behind a tree, Tiff sat down, idly watching the hide for the next half hour. She'd no idea what he was looking at. Yes, there were occasional birds and at one point, she thought she saw a small animal in the distance, though she could not identify it, but really, there was not a lot going on. Maybe he knew this as well because Bertrand left after thirty minutes.

His next port of call took him to a spot just on the edge of the compound, and Tiff saw him reach into his backpack, take out a tripod and a camera, and then put his binoculars around his neck. The man stared forward, his jutting chin barely making it past the fatty skin underneath it. He was quite a rotund man in a lot of ways, although he was nearly six-foot-tall, but he carried a weight with him. Tiff thought in some ways he was a pompous ass, but whatever he was looking at, he was obviously enjoying the view as he kept returning to his camera and then back up to his binoculars.

From her current place, it was hard for Tiff to see what he was looking at, as she was at right angles to him, hidden behind the trees. She wondered, could she get into a line of sight, and see with her bare eye what was so fascinating? Occasionally, he would wipe his mouth almost as if he were drooling, and Tiff thought about him eating some sort of large chicken, globules of fat falling down, wiping his hands clean. That's what he looked like to her, one of those unpleasant men in the films, the one who is always casting eyes at women, but not in that nice way. Almost like sizing them up. Cattle market, that's what Cat had called those places, wasn't it? Where men would look down on the women dressed up in the nightclubs, only a guy like this wouldn't be in a nightclub. It would be somewhere else. He would be the guy on the beach with binoculars. Tiff shivered, and it wasn't from the cold.

She needed to see what Bertrand was looking at. Carefully, Tiff started to walk away from him, getting a good distance but still keeping him in sight. She passed along through the wood, desperately trying not to step on any twig. At one point, he seemed to move frantically, starting to look around him as if he'd been seen. Tiff settled down behind the tree, keeping an eye on Bertrand until he settled again, and began firing shots with the camera. Once Tiff was directly behind him, she made her way in, lurking behind each tree, gradually getting closer and closer until the man was only twenty feet away. Whatever he was looking at, he needed binoculars. But he also needed a large telephoto lens on the camera. Maybe she could see well enough. Tiff peered out from behind a tree, staring.

She could see a chalet, a window. Which chalet it was, remained unclear, for they were all the same. On this side of the compound, it couldn't be Tiff's. It also couldn't be the students; neither could it be Gordon and Julie's. That only left Jodie's and the Roberts's, and Bertrand's. He was hardly going to be looking at his own chalet. And Jodie was still inside, apparently sleeping in Tiff's room for the day. So maybe it was the Roberts's. He'd been looking at Celia Roberts the other day and Tiff remembered him licking his lips, wiping the globules that were coming out on the back of his hand. She shivered again. She stared hard at the window and realized that the curtains were closed across it. What on earth was he doing looking at a curtain, getting excited? Tiff had heard about strange things in her time, but getting excited looking at a curtain from a distance, that really would be something.

Then the curtain flew back. There was a figure, and it was definitely female. The lack of clothing allowed for a clear decision about the sex of the individual. The curtain flew back across again. Tiff could see Bertrand was getting rather excited and then the curtain slid back again, this time for a longer period, and a dance was taking place. Tiff remembered those old James Bond films where they had a silhouette with a woman dancing provocatively. It was also on that program that the writer had done 'Tales of the Unexpected.' It was that sort of dancing that was going on all right. And then the curtain flew back again. Bertrand was clearly enjoying this.

Tiff was unsure who the woman was. She kept parading herself at the window and it was the Roberts's house. The woman was white-skinned, so it wasn't Jodie. It must be Celia. So, she knew about Bertrand. After all, who seriously went and danced in front of a window like that without knowing someone was looking.

Tiff held her position and watched as the curtain flew back and forward at least another six or seven times. Every time it seemed to be this dance and Bertrand seemed to be struggling to contain himself and then suddenly he was packing up. The curtain had closed and he was on the move. Tiff started to follow, but she was only thirty yards behind and then she stepped on a twig, the one she'd been dreading for the last hour, the one that sent a loud crack into the air.

Tiff didn't wait for Bertrand to look around, instead standing upright behind a tree and listening as best she as could for his movement. He didn't move far, for there was no crunching through the snow. There was nothing. Maybe he had the binoculars up to his face, checking, scanning the scenery behind. Tiff dared not move, her heart beating fast.

What would he do if he realized she'd been following him? Maybe that's what happened with Alice. Maybe she had followed him. Maybe she caught him, and he had disposed of her. The thought sent shivers down to her spine, and she felt her hands begin to shake. Did she really put herself in this position, thirty feet from a killer? If she had her board with her, she could soon get away. She'd find a slope; some sort of downhill patch and she would sail away from him. If only Cat was here, at least it would be two of them. She could maybe talk to him. Her aunt was good at that. She could talk to people; she could handle people. Not physically, never physically—she was quite weak in that department. But she could talk to them in a way Tiff envied. Every time Tiff spoke to someone, they took it the wrong way. They said she was arrogant, they said she wasn't listening, but she spoke perfectly normally, like anyone else. People just didn't listen right; it wasn't her fault. You couldn't blame her that people didn't understand her; she was speaking English, after all.

Lost in these thoughts, Tiff almost missed the crunching of the snow, as Bertrand stepped off in some direction. Was he coming towards her? If so, she had better come out running. Had he put a foot out to see if someone would look out. Surely it was best to look. Best to look and run if he noticed her, best to look and realize he was closer and get out of there. Standing still would not help, and if he saw her, he saw her.

Tiff tried to convince herself of this and then stuck her head out from behind the tree. Relief poured down on her as she saw Bertrand walking away. Still being cautious in case he looked around again, she threw herself behind the tree once more. Tiff was not moving until she saw the man at a decent distance from her, then she could follow. She heard the crunching of the snow, the feet lifting up and down, dropping in, and each time it seemed to be quieter. The next time she looked around the tree, he was nowhere to be seen.

Part of Tiff chastised herself. What sort of detective was she letting him go? But another part felt relieved. She walked over to the spot where the camera had stood and saw a clear path right through to the chalet. There was no curtain across the window, it was pulled back, and there was a woman there. He'd taken photographs; clearly, she must've been wanting him to. There was something going on between them, Bertrand

and Celia. Had Alice stumbled upon it?

Tiff made her way back to where Alice had been found. As she approached, she felt a chill in the air, and everything was quiet. There was barely a sign of the birds and the animals, but as she got closer to the scene of Alice's death, she swore even those signs were dropping away. Here, she was not that far from the compound. Here, she could even, if she were lucky, hear the sound of someone shouting or talking. Tiff thought she heard the kids playing, the two young boys from the chalet, just down from her own.

The ground around where Alice's body had been, was well trampled. Tiff could tell that was where the body was because Cat had described how Alice had been thrown forward off her skis, which were still stuck in the ground. This was clearly a preposterous idea. No one would crash like that, so why were the sticks there in the first place? Maybe the killer didn't know how to ski; maybe they didn't realize how silly the tableau they had created looked.

Tiff started to look towards the compound and she walked here and there, looking for a line through the trees where she could see any of the buildings. Finally, she found one. It was narrow, but it was clearly there. There was a window, but she couldn't work out which window it was and on what chalet. Turning back, she surveyed the scene of Alice's death again until she was happy that she could retain most of it in her head.

She turned and looked at the chalet window she had found, looked at the ground, wanting to see if there was any sign of a tripod. But the ground had been indented so much, it would be hard to tell if somebody had walked over here deliberately to hide tracks. Who knew, but Tiffany needed to know where the chalet was, so she turned and started walking on a direct line.

Here and there the terrain was rough, even an old stump hidden underneath the snow that she nearly tripped over, but Tiff was determined and kept walking straight to that window. Finally, she'd reached the edge of a line of trees, with the chalet some one hundred yards beyond, and then there was someone at the window. Tiff threw herself to the left, down behind another tree before looking back up.

Someone passed by that window again, and then the figure stopped and looked out, Tiff hoped she wasn't looking at her because she saw the face of Celia Roberts. The woman was fully dressed, but she seemed to have a smile on her lips. After a few moments Celia walked away, and Tiff stood up, walking away from the line of sight she'd been following. So was this it? Had it been that simple? Did Bertrand have a motive for murder? She'd seek out her aunt. Cat would know where to go from here; she'd have to.

Chapter 9

Tiff entered the chalet, but found that apart from Jodie, it was empty. The girl was still lying in the bed, covers wrapped up around her, shivering. Jodie was not as bad as she had been, but clearly, she was not that well. Tiff watched her from the bedroom door for a while before shouting over, 'Is there anything I can do for you?'

'Go away. Get me my entourage. Get them here. They have stuff. Get them to me.'

'That won't be for a few days. If you don't want anything, I'm away.' With that, Tiff turned on her heel and made for the main building to find her aunt. Tiff stood at the rear door, watching the bar area where she saw Cat downing some sort of cocktail. Who knew what sort of state she would be in? For such a sensible person at times, Cat seemed to like to drink a lot, something Tiff never did. What was the point of alcohol? All it did was get you stupid. A lot of these people were stupid enough to begin with—they didn't need any help. Cat wasn't stupid. Obviously, she wasn't as clever as Tiff, but stupid was not something Tiff associated with her. Strict, unseeing, slow-to-follow sensible and reasonable ideas from Tiff, but not stupid.

The other thing that was bothering Tiff was there was a dead body sitting in a nearby room, yet these people were acting like it was party time. Cat had mentioned things like a wake before, and Tiff reckoned there were definitely two different types of wake. One where everybody was incredibly sober, and the other one, when they just seemed to get drunk, telling stories of this and that, then laughing their heads off. This appeared to be the second type. Tiff made her way over and walked up behind Cat, who was sitting on a stool at the bar. She tapped her hand on her aunt's shoulder and Cat spun around.

'Oh, it's you. Where have you been? Somebody said you've been a good little camper, helping out.'

So, she was in that drunk patronizing mood, was she? thought Tiff. 'I need you now up to the chalet. We need to talk about something.'

'I'm just having a few drinks, just getting to know these people. You see that person there? This is Sarah. Sarah is studying biology. You could study biology, Tiff, but don't do what Alan's doing. He's an accountant. I mean good money, Tiff, in accountancy, but, oh, how dull is that? Biology, they cut people up.'

Tiff stared impassively at her aunt. 'I think it's time for your medication,' said Tiff.

'What medication?'

'Exactly. You can't even remember it. Come on.' Tiff grabbed Cat by the wrist, violently pulling her off the stool.

'Bye, everyone. I will speak to you later,' said Cat, as she half-stumbled along behind Tiff. Once outside, Tiff noticed that Cat seemed to get worse as she walked from side-to-side before Tiff took her by the hand and led her all the way up to the chalet. Once inside, Tiff helped her aunt plonk herself onto a chair and headed off to undo some flasks and make some instant coffee. She put three sugars into it, a drop of milk, and two spoonsful of the coffee. Taking it back to her aunt, she smiled and handed it over. Cat took one sip.

'Oh, this is vile. How strong is that? What's in that?'

'Get it down you. I need you sober until—listen, while you've been messing about and getting drunk, I've been out investigating, and I've found something.'

'You've found something? What do you think I was doing? I know all about these people now. I know'—Cat gave a little hick—'what makes them tick.'

'Well, you'd better tell me then so I can make a note of it before you forget.'

'Don't you come that with me. I'm your Aunt. I'm the older relative here. I'm the one showing sensible courses of action during all of this. Just step back and find yourself a bottle of water.' Tiff opened one, took a slow drink from it, and then placed it down before pulling over a chair and sitting in front of her aunt.

'Listen, I was just following Bertrand. I was doing the errands back and forward for Coralie and then I saw Bertrand when I went to deliver stuff to his door. Well, he's an arrogant sort of a thing and then he walked off, not even a thanks for what I was doing for him. So, I decided to follow him. Wait till you hear this. He goes out into the woods and he goes to a hide—half an hour, he does nothing but look at birds. Then he goes somewhere else and then he's looking at a different sort of bird.'

Cat swayed in her seat. 'What are you on about?'

'I saw him. He had a tripod, he had a camera, he had binoculars, and he was looking through the window at Celia Roberts.'

'So, he was spying on her?'

'No, he wasn't spying. I think this was deliberate. I think it was a mutual effort because she was at the window dancing, showing off.'

'What's wrong with standing at a window dancing, and if he took photographs of her dancing, what's wrong with that?'

'Because she didn't have anything on. She was well, you know, and he, the dirty pervert, was taking all these photographs. There's something going on between those two, but it got me thinking, what do you see? Look.' With that, Tiff walked over to her bedroom, quietly opening the door, and took out a pad of paper and a pen before closing the door gently behind her so as not to wake up Jodie. 'There're different lines of sight through the trees in the perimeter that lead to the windows in the chalets. If you look at these points,'—Tiff drew a rough outline of the area and put two crosses with two lines to a square representing a chalet—'that is where Bertrand was standing when he was taking these photographs, but the top one, that's back where Alice died. It's very close to it. So, I wondered, is that why she died? Did she find him?'

'If you think that he killed her, what were you doing?'

'I didn't know he killed her until I got there. I was just checking up and besides, I was incredibly quiet and kept out of the way. He never saw me.'

'Right, young lady, you don't go anywhere like that without me from now on, do you hear? We're not messing around anymore?'

'I'm fine,' said Tiff. 'I'm in a particularly good state of mind. You, however, are obviously drunk. Maybe I should wait until you sober up.'

'I'm perfectly well able to listen to you,' said Cat. 'Give me some of that water.' Tiff watched her aunt down the bottle of water and then, giving a sigh, went off to get another one. When Tiff returned with a second bottle of water, she made sure her aunt was focusing on her before continuing.

'I looked at where Alice was and the skis that were upright. It's a completely ludicrous idea that she crashed. She couldn't have been going any speed in that forest, anyway. There are no ski poles to propel herself along. It's like somebody just came up and just shoved the skis down into the ground like they needed a plan in a hurry. I think we need to go and look at Alice to see exactly how she died. They're saying a broken neck, but how? What sort of broken neck?'

'Tiff, what is it that everywhere we go you want to look at a dead body?'

'You have to look at the dead body. When you want to investigate, you need to know how people died. I'm not being unreasonable. Will you just listen to me and we can get to the bottom of this?'

'We? Oh, I'm included, am I? That's good to know. Well, listen, and listen up well because this is what socializing with people does for you. Well, you see the students—you have Debbie. She's the blonde-haired one. Debbie Kimble, I believe she's called. Her father is paying for this trip and she invited her friends along. Now, Alice was her friend and Kyle was Alice's boyfriend and they were shouting and getting on all the time. Debbie thinks something's going on with Kyle. She doesn't believe that Alice has been the only one he's been around. Apparently, he's been very friendly with others. Derek's become part of their crowd, Derek Lime. He's the one that looks rather, well drab, sullen. I think he's ill. Then there's Alan. Well, he's a bit older, so I'm not quite sure what's going on there, but Debbie likes Alan. That's why Alan got to come along. Sarah Lyons is Debbie's other friend. They all came out together except for Kyle. Kyle came because of Alice. It took a bit of a while working all that out. I tried to find out who was in when Alice was killed and I can't get anyone to say who was in and who was out. They were either in the room on their own or one or two of them said they were out. You got all that.'

'You said they were outside.'

'Well,' said Cat. 'Alan Edwards wasn't. He reckons he saw John Roberts outside as well disappearing off somewhere.'

'Did we not knock up the Roberts's when you left and I stayed here, cold and wanting to sleep?'

'Yes, we did. He wasn't there. It was only Celia, so that seems a bit strange to me.'

'It ties up what I'm thinking,' said Tiff. 'Maybe Celia was at the window doing her dancing whenever Alice caught them. John wasn't in the house. It makes sense. I think we'll get to the bottom of this nice and quick.'

'Tiff, you can't be like that. You have to have that, what do you call it? That thing. You need . . . '

'Evidence?' said Tiff. 'I know you need evidence. I've got a motive though.'

'You've got what you think is a motive. We need evidence, as I say. We need to go and check the body and see how she died. Maybe Gordon can help us.'

Tiff stood up, turned her back with a tut. She heard her aunt shout over her shoulder. 'What's that for? What's wrong when I mention his name?'

'You don't have a great track record when it comes to picking men to help us investigate things, do you?'

'We've had one time when we've had to look into something. If you remember rightly, I gave him a good swift knee to the family jewels in the end. Didn't like him. He really was slime, wasn't he?'

'You can't be trusted with that sort of judgment. Therefore, I think we go alone. We do it on our own. Now's a good time to go down as well,' said Tiff, 'because all the students are drunk. There's nobody else down there except Denis and Coralie. I'm sure you can find a way of getting Denis out of the way. That guy jumps at anything. Will probably listen to anything you say to him.'

Tiff turned around and saw her aunt stand up. 'Get me another bottle of water and a couple of paracetamol; then we start to do this.'

'Don't you want to sober up a bit first?' said Tiff.

'If I sober up anymore, I'll not do it. Unlike you, I don't have a desire to want to see dead bodies. For the record, that's a pretty morbid thing to be looking out for.'

Tiff shook her head and waited while her aunt drank another bottle of water, took two paracetamol, and then could be heard splashing some of the water around her face. 'Let's go,' said Cat, and marched forward before tripping slightly and stumbling. 'I'm fine. Let's go.'

Tiff watched her aunt walk out of the room. Part of her wasn't completely sure that she was totally with it, but that might be a good thing. Plenty of distraction for other people while Tiff moved about. The cool air this time seemed to do something for Cat. Tiff noticed that she was walking a lot straighter by the time they reached the main building again. Alice's body was in a room off to one side, and Tiff wanted to make sure the door was not locked. She whispered in her aunt's ear to go over to the main desk to talk to Denis while Tiff walked past and checked the door.

Once she saw her aunt engaged with the man, Tiff casually strolled past, put out her hand, pressed down, and pushed. The door was open, but Tiff didn't push it too far so that it could close gently back. Continuing her walk, she turned into the ladies' toilets. When she came back out two minutes later, she saw her aunt sitting down by the fire, warming her back. Denis was coming over.

'I was just telling Denis we needed a bite to eat,' said Cat. 'Something's got to soak up all that alcohol I've just drunk.'

'Yes. Some bread, perhaps. Something. A sandwich. Something of that nature.'

'Ideal, Denis. Good idea. Why don't you pop in and make it? What do you want, Tiff?'

'Give me a couple of boiled eggs,' said Tiff. With that, Denis nodded and headed off.

'You don't even like boiled eggs,' said Cat.

'No,' said Tiff, 'but they do take a while to cook. Now, come on. Over we go.'

'But the other people are still here at the bar. Look, there're the students.'

'And they're as drunk as anything. Don't worry about them,' said Tiff. 'Come on, over we go. Just act normal.'

Tiff stood up and let her aunt walk first. There was still a slight zigzagging with the lines as Cat made her way to the door behind which the body of Alice lay. It was a games' room and inside on a table tennis table, the corpse had been laid covered over with various blankets. As her aunt opened the door, Tiff could see her shake slightly. She was always so queasy around death. The woman was dead. Alice wasn't going to do anything, but her body had plenty to tell them and that was the key. Cat stepped inside and Tiff followed, shutting the door behind her but looking out through the small glass window. She couldn't see anyone looking over and thought that they must have got away with it.

'You stand at the door, then you can blag anyone that comes in. I'm going to have a quick look,' said Tiff.

'Maybe I should look as well,' said Cat.

'Last time you couldn't even tell that the guy wasn't dead,' said Tiff. 'I'll do it. There's no point you looking at her. Who knows what you'll come up with?' Tiff saw Cat roll her eyes at her, but her aunt turned around and stood facing the door.

'Get on with it then,' she said. Tiff moved the blankets back and saw the woman lying there, her skin pale. The eyes were closed, possibly because someone pulled them down and Tiff ran her hands around the neck area. She tried to lift the body up slightly and felt the weight of the head tipping back. Carefully, she pulled up the jumper the girl was wearing and saw a number of bruises around her ribs. Pulling down the trousers, she also saw bruising on the legs, and the shins, and the knees. Tiff turned her over and saw strap-like marks across her bare buttocks. It was all a bit strange, but clearly, there was some sort of level of abuse with the girl. Either that or she liked a lot of pain. *You never knew people until you really got to know them, until you live with them.* She'd heard that somewhere. She couldn't remember if it were a famous detective or not, but the tale was right.

Tiff carefully pulled up the girl's trousers and then moved her back into position before pulling her jumper down. It was then she noticed the jaw possibly not being completely in line. She ran her hands around it and heard a click as it fell off to one side, moving over maybe an inch. It was clearly broken to some degree. There was also heavy bruising in and under the jaw and around the back of the neck. Tiff couldn't be totally sure, but that didn't look like the neck had been broken in an accident. It looked like somebody had put pressure around it to break it. She'd seen enough, and they needed to get moving again. Carefully, she took the blanket and moved it back over the body. It had been time well spent and she felt she'd learnt something about the girl.

'Are you done?' asked Cat.

'Yes, I'm done. Let's get out of here.'

'What did you find? Tell me what you found. You can't tell me out there.'

'The neck's broken, probably by somebody. She's got a lot of bruising on her and she's got strap marks across her buttocks. Something isn't right. She'd either had a lot of abuse or she enjoys a bit of the rough stuff.'

'How do you know about the rough stuff?' demanded Cat, and then they heard the door behind them click open.

Chapter 10

'What are you doing in here?' asked Coralie. 'No one should be in here.' The woman looked over at Tiff. 'Have you been anywhere near that body? Have you been having a proper look? Why? What are you doing? Are you trying to cover up your tracks? I wondered why you were befriending me today.'

'Befriend you? Tiff was befriending you,' said Cat. 'Oh, that's genuine; Tiff doesn't make friends with anybody easily. If she's making friends with you, she genuinely wants to be friends.'

'That still doesn't answer what you're doing in here.' Coralie fixed them with a hard stare and Cat began to smile. She reckoned Tiff could probably see her shaking foot but Coralie couldn't. Tiff raised her hand smoothing her pony tail out behind her.

'We're just investigating,' said Cat. 'Something's amiss here. This girl didn't die naturally.'

'Do you think I've ever seen a ski accident like that? I don't know what Denis is thinking, but that still doesn't answer what you're doing in here. How do we know you didn't commit the murder?'

'Me?' said Cat in complete disbelief. 'Why? What have I got against her? I don't even know her. First I saw of her was in here when she was having a blazing row with that man of hers and as for Tiff here, there's not a bad bone in her body. Half the time Tiff might not be in this world but she's certainly not for killing people.'

Coralie stepped inside and closed the door behind her. 'Just say I assume that you're telling me the truth, what makes you think you can come in and investigate? Why don't you just put a hold on everything? Nobody is going anywhere. Nobody is going to run off, we're stuck halfway up a mountain. We're lucky we've got food and we've got some warmth—other than that, there's nowhere to go. It's best to sit and wait for the police to get here. Let them solve it.'

'You're happy to sit here while there's a murderer about. Why?' asked Cat. 'Doesn't that scare you? How do you know they're not going to come for you?'

'I had nothing to do with Alice,' said Coralie in a whisper. 'Why would they come for me?'

'Why would they go for her?' said Tiff. 'We don't know, we need to investigate, we need to know. Maybe it's women they're after, maybe we're at risk. Maybe the men are fine. Maybe it's just someone who likes to kill.'

'Enough, Tiff,' said Cat. 'Don't make this melodramatic; it's bad enough as it is. It's not the first time we've seen a body,' said Cat raising her shoulders up as if she owned the place. 'Last time, we worked out what happened, so I think it's only fair that we take charge.'

'Take charge? Woah, easy. I'm not having somebody running around like this. You're a guest. If you're going to end up in the same situation as Alice, I'll be for it. No, that's not on; you're my responsibility.'

'I'm Denis's responsibility as well,' said Cat, 'but let's face it, if we leave it up to him we could all be dead by sunset. He couldn't find his own underpants in the washing, never mind a killer in here.'

'Hang on a minute anyway; you were sitting drinking with all those students. You don't look like somebody suitable to investigate.'

'I was getting close, that's all.'

'She's still tipsy,' said Tiff, 'but she did it. Aunt Cat knows all about them now. She's good at that. I'm the brains but she's the social dynamo.'

Cat turned around and gave Tiff a wink. 'Do you really think that?' Tiff simply stared back. You couldn't expect to get a compliment and then have Tiff back it up with anything else. Cat turned back to Coralie.

'Look, you can be in with us. I understand you're worried and I understand you want to look after the guests. So, work with us, not against us.'

'Do you know anything about dead bodies?' said Coralie.

'I don't,' said Cat, 'but Tiff does. She's looked, and she's confirmed that the neck was probably broken by someone, not from a fall. As you said before, those skis were completely in the wrong position.'

'So, who did it then?'

'We have suspicions,' says Cat, 'but we need to develop them into evidence, not simply theories. We also need to know more about other groups. That's why I was speaking with the students. That's why I'm getting in with them. Tiff's been working to follow Bertrand around and she's found some rather strange practices of his. We haven't got close yet to the Roberts or the Plymouths. We kind of neglected them today; maybe you could do that. I don't feel right walking up half-cut to a family with kids.'

'You do know that they're not his kids; that's his sister?'

'She's well aware of that,' said Tiff. 'She was well pleased.' Cat shot a look over to Tiff before turning back to Coralie. 'I think it's probably best you speak to them. You can go over there saying you're here to help and assist with the kids, keep them entertained and out of the way during all this madness.'

'But we need to be careful,' said Coralie. 'If anyone actually gets wind of what we're up to, we could tip them into doing something shocking.'

'Or running,' said Tiff, 'there's always that. Still, you and I could ski after them.'

'It's not a Hollywood movie,' said Cat. 'We talked about this before. You are not the one to charge around.'

'Well, you charged around last time; you dived into the sea to save people. But you're rubbish on the snow; therefore, this is my domain. This is where I can excel. I can pick up that side this time.'

'No,' said Cat, 'I didn't pick it up last time. It just happened, so enough of that.'

'I've got to get back to Denis, he's still working on your meals and he knows nothing but it's not him. He loves this place, loves his job. There would be no reason for him to do it. He can only look bad from this. Trust me, I know him, it's not him.'

'I doubt very much it was him,' said Cat. 'He doesn't look the type. Secondly, he doesn't look that he's got the power or ability. He certainly couldn't plan it out. Although, how planned out it was, I'm not sure. Tiff, tell Coralie about Bertrand.' Tiff quickly ran through her little excursion with Bertrand that day.

'Ooh, saucy,' said Coralie. 'Certainly wouldn't find me doing that for a guy, especially one like him. He's a bit of a weirdo.'

'But is he a weirdo?' said Cat. 'Or is he a killer? That's the real question.'

'It would be hard to prove that she stumbled on him and he did it,' said Tiff. 'There was nothing else around when we found her, was there?'

'No,' said Cat, 'not that I could tell, but it's been walked on since then. I didn't see the snow prints, I didn't see that. Who knew what shoe marks were there, what people could have done? But Denis brought everybody in to move the body. Tiff was out there and she could have picked up a little from it. She's good at those things. Whatever else you think of my niece, she's good at those things.'

'She certainly knows how to handle a snowboard. Right, I think we need to meet up later. I'll find a way to get with the Plymouths, talk to them, and I'll talk to the Roberts as well. I'll see if I can worm out of Celia what's going on. One thing I had noticed about them is she doesn't tend to bother with her husband.'

'True,' said Cat. 'Right. We'll go back and we'll sit and eat our meal, and Tiff will get off doing a bit more snooping, and I'll get over with the students, see what else I can discover from them. We also better drop back and see Jodie. That's somebody else you can look at, Tiff. Maybe Jodie will speak to you; she's not going to go far, and you certainly will be able to talk to her easier than me.'

'Why is that?' asked Tiff.

'Because you can be as ignorant as you want to her. She's a diva, and all she wants is her own way. Speak to her how you want. It'll annoy her.'

'But I might not get much out of her,' said Tiff.

'You can do it,' said Cat. 'I believe in you. Come on, let's go eat our meal, and then off you go.' The three women exited the room with Cat and Tiff taking up their seats, while Coralie headed back towards the kitchen. Denis appeared shortly with some stew, and Cat devoured it greedily. That was the thing about alcohol, it always made you hungry. Too much, and it made you hungry for things that weren't food as well; she'd have to be careful. These students were knocking drinks back like anything, which she would happily do if she were simply out for a good time. But now she needed to discover truths, and she'd already drunk plenty that day.

After they finished their meal, Cat gave Tiff a nod and wandered off towards the students, leaving Tiff to return up to their chalet. A light snow had begun to fall when Tiff got outside, but the cloud cover was still thick, and Tiff doubted anyone would arrive to help them within the next couple of days. Stepping inside the chalet, Tiff felt it to be slightly cold, and when she went inside, she found the fire had died right down. Taking the basket outside, she filled it up with some logs before returning and getting the fire going. It spat and crackled, and Tiff made herself a hot chocolate, before sitting down in the warmth of the burning logs. She placed her earphones in and started listening to her music. Before she realized it, the bedroom door was opening.

Jodie was standing there with Tiff's dressing gown around her.

'You've got the fire going, that's good. I needed warmed up. I didn't want to get up until someone had made the fire.' Tiff ignored her. 'Did you hear me? I said I didn't want to get up.'

'Fine, suits me.' Tiff put her head back down again listening to her music.

'Can you get me some food?' There was no response from Tiff, and then Jodie tapped her on the shoulder causing Tiff to look up, taking out one of the earphones. 'I said, can you get me some food?'

'Why? Can't you get it?'

'I don't get the food; it's brought to me. That's what I pay people for.'

'You don't pay me. You never said you would pay me. How much would you pay people to get food?'

Jodie stared at Tiff. 'Go and get me some food. I'm hungry.'

'I'm not,' said Tiff. 'I went down with Cat, and we got some food. It was quite nice. You should go down and get some food.'

'I asked you to get the food. I expect to be waited on. Do you know who I am?'

Tiff looked up at her. 'You're Jodie. You sing.'

'That's right. You can see my face on album covers everywhere, on posters, I sell out crowds and halls and stadiums, and then I end up here and they clear off and they leave me. Now go and get me some food.'

'Do you know who I am?' said Tiff. Jodie shook her head. 'I'm Tiffany. I sit here and I put my earphones in and I listen to music. That's what I'm doing. I don't get food.' With that, Tiff bent her head down again. Jodie marched off, slamming the bedroom door behind her and Tiff watched as she appeared five minutes later, clothed in a snowsuit. It was Tiff's spare and it was slightly large on Jodie, which was impressive because Tiff was by no means a sizable girl. Jodie marched up in front of her, announced she was going to get some food, and Tiff simply nodded, which seemed to cause major ructions. It was twenty minutes later when Jodie came back into the chalet.

'Why is your sister just drinking with those people?'

'Because she likes to drink. She's not my sister; she's my aunt.'

'Aunt? They're meant to be older, aren't they?'

'She is old,' said Tiff. 'I think she's six years older than me. She's in her twenties. She's incredibly old.'

The woman stared at Tiff. 'Are you simple?'

Tiff looked back. 'No. I'm quite clever, actually. I can make my own food as well. I can go about on my own, and I don't need people to look after me. Can you do that or are you simple?' The comment came without malice, and that was because there was none intended. Tiff never saw the world like that. Never saw a way to retaliate like that. Instead, she stated it as she saw it, which is probably the most brutal way of telling things to people who didn't want to hear. 'Why did you run off the other night?'

'I needed something,' said Jodie. 'I needed something and nobody brought it to me so I had to go and get it.'

'Did you find it,' asked Tiff, 'what you were looking for?' Jodie nodded. 'My sister thinks you do drugs. Do you?'

'Of course, I do drugs. Tell me you've never had any drugs. You've never taken cocaine. You've never stuck a needle in your arm?'

'No,' said Tiff. 'I don't drink alcohol either. It makes you silly, like drugs. I don't need drugs.'

'You can say that, sister,' said Jodi; 'you're crackers as it is.'

'Are you going to sit down? Or are you going to wander about in a snow suit in here because it's going to get quite warm,' said Tiff. With that, Jodie stormed off to the bedroom before coming back out in Tiff's dressing gown. 'You don't tend to wear a lot,' said Tiff, 'about the place. Is that normal?'

'Well, yes,' said Jodie. 'They do like a bit of flesh on the covers, don't they?'

'What covers?' said Tiff. 'Oh, you mean the music. I don't know. I don't really look at the covers,' she said. 'I listen to the music. That's the bit I like. The music bit. Never heard your stuff though.' With that, Tiff put her head back down. Jodie was fuming, not that Tiff noticed.

'Do you think we can get out of here?' said Jodie.

Tiff raised her head. 'No. We're closed in. Do you need more drugs?'

'Yes,' she said. 'Can you tell?'

'Well, you do start to shake sometimes. You're not as bad as you were the other night. I just don't understand where you're getting them from up here. Do the students do them?'

'I don't know,' said Jodie. 'You don't really tell people who you get them from, do you, because if they find out you've told people you won't get them back again.'

'You're all right with me,' said Tiff. 'I won't tell anyone. I don't need them. My aunt doesn't do them either. She might knock back the alcohol like there's no tomorrow, but she doesn't do drugs. Says they're silly and I agree with her.'

'But you're not under the pressure I'm under. I have to perform all the time, have to get up and be someone. You don't have to be anyone.'

Tiff stared hard at Jodie as if she were thinking about something. 'I have to be Tiff every day. It's not easy being Tiff. People don't understand me. I think it's because I'm far cleverer than them. They just don't see my world. It's like I'm an alien. It's like I'm from some other planet. They just don't get me.' Tiff watched Jodie look at her, questioning with her eyes as if she were taking the mick out of her. 'I'm being serious and that's what I get. All the time I get these people looking at me as if I'm not being serious. It's like I'm not on the right planet, like I fell here from somewhere else.'

'Sister, you fell here all right.'

'Last night, how did you end up in the hide?' asked Tiff.

'Because it was cold. It was cold out there. I didn't have much on when I went. That was my fault. Well, no, it wasn't my fault. Nobody gave me a coat. Nobody gave me a jacket. Nobody got my drugs for me. I had to go out and find them.'

'You're not used to that, are you?' said Tiff. 'I feel sorry for you. It can't be easy being you.'

'No, it's not,' said Jodie. 'I'm glad you realize that.'

'Oh, I do,' said Tiff. 'I've got talent. I'm fortunate.' Jodie turned around and marched back to the bedroom, slamming the door behind her. Tiff looked up and wondered what was wrong with the woman.

Chapter 11

Cat had been sitting at the bar for over an hour with the students, drinking but struggling to get any meaningful conversation out of them. When Derek suggested they head back to the chalet because he had some better things to be drinking than what was down at the bar, the rest had half cheered and began to trudge their way back up. Cat had insisted she would pick up a bottle of her own stuff before joining them.

The mood had been tense. Yes, there had been laughs, there had been jokes, but she had also seen petty comments and a number of glances that certainly had malice behind them. Returning briefly to her own chalet, Cat emptied a bottle of Vodka down the sink before filling it up from the tap with water. *Clear head,* she thought, *need to keep a clear head.* She made her way over to the students' chalet, banging on the door when she found it locked. It took another minute before Debbie opened the door, apologizing profusely that she had locked it accidentally.

The chalet was an extended copy of Cat's and one of her first thoughts was to reckon where everyone was sleeping. There were three bedrooms in total and one was extremely small. In her head, Cat tried to pair up the students. Alice Tarney had been with Kyle Cobbler; that much was evident, so maybe they shared a room. But did Debbie and Sarah have a separate room from Derek and Alan, or were they together as couples? Who with whom? Cat smiled as she walked into the room and gave her head a little shake, trying to clear it. She needed to focus.

'Whoa,' said Alan, 'vodka. Looking to mix something up?'

'Neat,' said Cat. 'I take it neat.' Then she grinned intensely as she saw Alan's face.

'You're quite something, aren't you? I mean I was expecting some sort of hoity-toity woman but not you. You're mixing it with the best of them.'

'A bottle like that needs a glass like this,' said Derek Lane, placing a tall, thin shot glass in front of Cat. 'Go on, show me how you handle it.'

Cat undid the bottle, poured in a full measure, and knocked it back. There was a light cheer as Cat made the water disappear down her throat. It was almost too easy, but then again many of them were so drunk they probably wouldn't realize if they were drinking water themselves.

Kyle was sitting in the middle of the room, almost oblivious of the scene behind him. Sarah Lyons was rubbing his shoulders. Cat noticed that Alan watched very closely, and she recognized the jealousy in his face. Meanwhile, a pair of hands began to rub her shoulders, and she turned her head to look up into the face of Derek Lyon.

'You are certainly one for a good time, aren't you?' With that, she felt him begin to rub her neck across the back and tussle her hair.

'Are you the provider of a good time, Derek?'

'Is it only liquids you take? If you want, I might be able to provide you with something else.'

Cat reached forward and took her vodka bottle, pulling it to herself. 'This is my man, Derek. He can drink with me, he can laugh with me, but this bottle here is who goes to bed with me.'

It was cheesy and she saw the look of disappointment on his face. Especially when Debbie came over and slapped him on the side, laughing at how he'd bombed so badly making his pass.

'I can't believe you,' said Alan suddenly, his face intense.

'You can't believe what?' said Debbie, stroking her hand through her blonde hair. Cat thought she had all the trappings of a little rich girl. The friends around her hanging on, no doubt drinking away everything her father had provided. Someone who was at the centre of the group soaking up any attention that was given.

'Kyle, look at him; he'll be in bed with Sarah by tonight.'

Sarah let go of Kyle's shoulders, walked over and slapped Alan across the face.

'Oh, oh,' said Derek, 'here we go.'

Kyle tried to rise up from a seated position to his feet but was stumbling badly. 'Just you leave Sarah alone. She's told you already. She's not interested, Alan. Not interested at all.'

Alan stepped up close to Kyle's face. 'And you,' he said, 'your woman's only dead and you're still trying to get into bed with someone else. Look at you. You disgust me.'

Kyle took a swing, missed completely, and fell over on the floor. 'Hey, hey,' said Debbie. 'Easy. What the heck do you think you're doing? I'm not going to be having any fighting in here.'

'I wouldn't fight that,' said Alan. Then landed a kick right into the guts of Kyle. It caused the man to roll over up onto his knees, where he proceeded to vomit on the floor.

'Bloody hell,' said Debbie. 'Enough. Who the hell's going to clean that up?'

'Denis, of course,' said Derek. 'That's what the little gnome's for. Shall I give the buzzer a press now?'

'Not until we give him something proper to clean up,' said Alan and delivered a kick to the face of Kyle. The man tumbled backwards onto the floor, blood coming from his mouth. Cat found herself launching out of her chair, putting her hands up in front of Alan, shouting, 'Alan. Stop it. No need for that.'

'What the hell do you know? He just swanned in. You didn't even treat her right. Did you? No wonder Alice was all over you. Shouting at you, complaining. Any woman going past is good enough for you. Don't know how to look after a woman.' With that, Alan launched another kick into Kyle's guts. Catriona could tell the situation was going to get messy quickly. She wondered why no one else seemed to be leaping in. Outside of Alan, she was probably the oldest person in the room, making her feel a bit like mum.

'Where were you when Alice died? Where were you, Kyle? You weren't here. I was here. You weren't. Was she just becoming a little too annoying? Needed to get rid of her, did you?'

'There's no need for those sorts of accusations,' said Debbie.

'Why?' said Alan. 'Why? We're all standing there drinking. We're all going around talking, having a laugh, and she's dead. She's lying down there in that other building, dead. Come to think of it. You weren't in here either. It was only me and Sarah in here. You weren't here. Derek was God knows where. Poor Alice was getting done in by someone at the same time.'

'It's an accident,' said Debbie. Alan started to laugh.

'An accident? It's the most pathetic-looking accident I've ever seen. It's only that little gnome that believes it. Everyone else knows something was up. Everyone else knows someone killed her. Even you do, don't you, Contessa?'

Cat now found everyone staring at her as if she was required to validate the statement. 'Easy,' said Cat. 'Everyone just calm down. The police will be here in a couple of days. They'll sort out what it was. Calm down. Have a drink. Here, Alan.' Cat turned around, took the bottle of vodka, and poured another shot before handing it to Alan. He looked at it almost with contempt.

'How is this going to solve anything? Look at him. Sarah, look at him,' said Alan, grabbing Sarah's arm and pulling her head down towards Kyle lying on the floor. 'You want to be with that instead of me? Fine. You can have it.' Alan stormed out of the room and Cat watched Sarah bend down to Kyle, rubbing his back before stepping away quickly as the man vomited again.

'That was all a bit overwrought, wasn't it?' said Cat. 'Is he just nuts or is he right? Those two, well, are those two together?'

Debbie looked at Cat, shaking her shoulders—Derek too—before Cat spun around and gave a questioning glance to Sarah.

'Alice tried to change him. Alice always wanted him to be a little Mr. Perfect. She didn't like his drinking. She didn't like a lot about him. Hell, I don't know why she was with him. She was no fun for him. Isn't that right, Kyle?'

Kyle spat some sick out onto the floor. When he looked up, his eyes were bloodshot, his hair a mess from the sweat and convulsions. 'She never liked a good time. Even here, she didn't want to come. She wasn't like you, a girl who likes to drink, a girl who's quite happy to mix it up a bit.'

Mix it up a bit? thought Cat, *how dare he? I think I've got a bit more class than that.* 'Where were you when Alice was out there?'

'I didn't know she was out there,' spat Kyle. 'I was just getting some quiet time with Sarah.'

'In that cold?' said Cat.

'We weren't there. We were in the main building at the time. I might like a wild time, but it would freeze the bits off you out there.'

Cat almost smirked at the comment. She also wondered if he was telling the truth. Denis and Coralie would have been down at the main building. *Where on earth had they gone to get their privacy? Where had Kyle taken Sarah or were they simply covering up?*

'Besides, no one was here,' said Kyle. 'Alan said it. Debbie and Derek weren't even here.' Cat spun around looking at them and she saw Debbie put her hand into Derek's. 'Well, everybody likes a bit of me-time. It is quite fun out there. Isn't it? Especially with the hides and the little getaway. My father gives me the chalet, but it's not as fun, is it? It's more fun to be out in the open.' Inside, Cat was a little shocked, but on the outside face, she maintained her cool stare.

'It's not good though, is it? Look at the state of this place. You better get yourselves together if the police show up, because at the moment, with the state of you, you'll be the ones they'll be focused on. No, I don't think it was an accident. I think no one but Denis thinks it was an accident.' Cat stood looking around as if she'd ended on a non-dramatic note. If this was one of those TV detectives, they would have said something pertinent before the scene cut away.

Instead, Cat found herself marching back over to pick up her glass that Alan had dumped on the way out. She filled it again and downed a shot followed by another one, much to the admiration of Derek. 'Well, it's all gone a bit flat,' said Cat. 'I'm going to retire, but seriously, guys, get your stuff together because the police aren't going to like this. Your stories better be watertight.' Grabbing her bottle and glass, Cat walked out of the front door, into the snow and immediately saw Alan to her left. The man was in tears, starting to cry, half hunched over.

'You all right?' asked Cat, putting an arm on his shoulder.

'Do I bloody look all right? That ignorant kid in there took Alice for a ride, and he's going to do the same with Sarah. What is it with you women? You always go with a good time guy. You don't go with a guy who could give you something steady.'

'That's a bit judgmental on the whole of womankind, isn't it?' said Cat. 'Here, have a go at this,' and she poured him a glass of vodka cum water and watched as the man downed it. Maybe he had drunk too much already because to Cat, it was obvious the liquid was water, yet the man licked his lips as if he'd taken some of the best Russian vodka available.

'When you said there was no one in here—what time was that?'

'Well,' said Alan, 'I don't know the time but they banged the door. It wasn't long before they banged on the door. I'd just woken up, came stumbling through. Kyle and Alice had been rowing earlier on, and I'd heard them. I think I heard her go out the door but didn't hear anyone else go out. When I woke up, someone banged on the door. I ran around the house trying to get everyone else. No one was here. I wasn't surprised that Debbie was out. Her and Derrick have been tight since we came here.'

'How do you all know each other?'

'We are at university together. Most of us. Derek isn't. Debbie knows Derek from somewhere else. To be honest, he's a wee bit quiet and creepy, but the rest of us were in halls together in our first year, not anymore. I still can't believe that Alice went with Kyle. Maybe three years now they've been together. She was never happy. I think maybe she thought she couldn't do any better. She was wrong there.

'I wasn't interested before you ask. I can see that look in your eyes. But other guys were, yet she still went with him. I think he was good at that stuff, calming a woman down, bringing her around, whatever that stuff is that does it. Wears thin after a time, doesn't it?'

'I wouldn't know,' said Cat, 'I've never had a man long enough to find that out.'

Alan turned to her. 'I didn't take you to be a girl like that, jumping in and out of any bed.'

Cat gave him a slap across the face, fairly gentle, but it got the point across. 'Don't speak to me like that. I'm not one of those girls. I'm a widow.' She saw the man's hurt look and in truth, she realized it had been a bit much. Maybe it was the alcohol causing her to snap. Something about that comment made her feel like she had disrespected Luigi. He'd have liked somewhere like this, somewhere inside one of the cabins. Skiing through the day, hit the bar at night with Cat, and back for some quiet time. She could feel a tear almost forming and had to force herself back to the task at hand.

'Do any of you know anyone else here?'

'I don't,' said Alan. 'We only came here because of Debbie.

Her father's paid for it all and he's stinking rich. Sorry, I didn't mean that. I didn't mean to sound antagonistic towards you. Particularly good of him to pay for all this, I guess. You've probably got money, haven't you? I didn't mean to imply that there was something wrong with it.'

'It's okay,' said Cat, trying to bring out her tender side, to see if the man would open up even more.

'Yes, I don't think anyone knows anybody else here. We've stuck to ourselves, mainly. The only person I've seen speak at all was Derek, to Bertrand, and that other guy, the Roberts man. He spoke to him a few times, but nothing that would suggest he knew them. Other than that, we've been pretty tight as a group. You've done well to make your way in, but you've got that about you, haven't you? That face. It's quite something.'

Cat smiled at the man and Alan placed a hand on her cheek as he gazed into her eyes.

'Thank you for the compliment, Alan, but like I said, I'm a widow and I'm not looking for anything like that.' Gently, she took his hand from her face and she saw a guy who never got the girl. He was probably pretty decent, probably the one the girls talked to when they wanted a serious conversation, but he didn't look fun. As the song went, 'Girls just want to have fun.' *Well, up to a point*, thought Cat. 'Here,' she said, 'You can finish the bottle.'

Chapter 12

Tiff was feeling great. Maybe it was because Cat had basically given her a part in the investigation. She had treated her like an equal, herself and Coralie. Coralie was quite something, someone that could ski and take charge, two things that Tiff valued in the world. When Coralie had taken her out on the board, she'd been able to impress Coralie with her turns and twists and overall command of the board, and Coralie had been quick to heap praise on Tiff. Often when Tiff spoke to people they didn't understand her, but maybe it was because they were speaking about the boarding, that Coralie and her they seemed to get on well. Coralie didn't ask any stupid questions, didn't bother Tiff about when she was getting up or what she was doing. She understood that the boarding was the important thing at the moment, nothing else—oh, and this investigation. So, it was good that she was involved now, but Tiff had been trusted with her own section of it.

Having initially engaged Jodie at the chalet, Tiff was resting up with her headphones on. Jodie had gone back to the bedroom, but a while later, Tiff heard the girl come back through the door.

'Oh, it's you. You haven't got anything to drink, have you?'

Of course, it's me, thought Tiff. *We only spoke a while ago. She must be gone.* 'The drinks in every chalet,' said Tiff. 'In the cabinet in there, and you pay for it afterwards. Did you not realize that?'

'I don't get my own drinks; people get them for me. Do you know how to make cocktails?'

'I don't drink,' said Tiff, 'I did say. And if I did, I'm not making you one. Look at you, you need your bed, not a cocktail.'

'Why can't you just do what I ask?' With that, Jodie stormed off back to the bedroom. She was still wearing Tiff's dressing gown and was beginning to annoy Tiff. *Why couldn't she go back to her own place and pick stuff up? I mean, how pathetic was this girl?*

Tiff paused from her listening for a moment because she needed to think out what she was going to do. Her job was to investigate Bertrand and Jodie. At the moment, Jodie wasn't that easy to investigate, as all she did was lounge around in her dressing gown looking for stuff. Clearly, she needed something. Tiff had seen Cat occasionally in the morning get up after having had a number of drinks the night before, and have what she called the hair of the dog. It was like she was withdrawing from the alcohol and she needed more of the same. Tiff had no idea how that felt, having never drunk alcohol in her life, but it seemed to be a weakness in people. She didn't need it.

Maybe it was a comfort blanket, like Cat's hairbrush. Whenever she was edgy or struggling with something, Cat would brush her hair. It was bizarre. Jodie seemed to need a lot of comfort blankets. Whatever it was she was looking for, she certainly wasn't of sound mind. Part of Tiff thought she should stay, look after the girl, make sure she didn't go running off anywhere, but she couldn't really do that. After all, Jodie was her own person. It was up to her what she did, not up to Tiff.

Tiff thought about her other suspect, Bertrand. She wondered if he was in his chalet. How would she know? She could hide somewhere and observe it, see if he was in his accommodation, mooching about. He was such a strange man. Maybe she wouldn't see him at the windows, but if she knocked on the door, he'd have to answer. That would be the best idea.

Delighted with this plan, Tiff stood up, got into her snowshoes, and made her way across to Bertrand's chalet. She thumped on the front door and stepped back down the steps, waiting for him to appear. After a minute of standing, Tiff stepped back up to the door and rapped on it again. Resuming her previous position, she waited again for the door to open. It took another thirty seconds and then slowly, the door was pulled back and there was Bertrand standing all in black, wearing a pair of sunglasses despite being indoors.

'What do you want?'

Tiff looked up and smiled at him. 'Do you have any toilet roll?'

'What? Do I have what?' Bertrand's English was good, but it was not perfect. Maybe this was one of the words that he didn't know. Tiff understood that happened when you learned languages. You could speak quite fluently, but you just didn't grasp what a word was. Maybe he'd never been to England asking for the toilet roll. Some people got embarrassed about anything to do with the toilet.

'Toilet roll,' said Tiff. 'I need some toilet roll. You wipe your bum with it.' Tiff provided a demonstration. The man shook his head. Tiff wished she could see his eyes, but they were hidden behind the sunglasses.

'Just a moment.' He disappeared back into his chalet and handed over a half-used toilet roll to Tiff. 'Don't disturb me again. I'm going out.' With that, the door was closed.

Who hands someone a half-used toilet roll? thought Tiff. *Only if it was your last one.* She made her way back to her own chalet, depositing the toilet roll on the table in the lounge before stepping back outside. If Bertrand was going out, she would need to tail him. Now equipped with her coat and snowshoes, she marched off into the woods beside the compound. Locating herself behind a tree, she was able to see the front door of Bertrand's house. It was only a five-minute wait before the man emerged, complete with backpack, black outfit, and sunglasses. Tiff watched him take up a stride she'd become familiar with. He didn't seem to be worried about anyone watching him as he marched off into the woods. Previously he'd seemed quite coy, but now he seemed almost carefree.

The path he took was a similar one to the previous, and he returned to the first hide she'd seen him in. A half-hour later he emerged from it and Tiff was glad to be on the move again, the cold starting to affect her. It was okay when you were snowboarding. You were on the move, the heat generated, finding a way to warm you. But when you had to sit and do nothing, and you couldn't even see the man inside the hide, you got a little fed up and cold.

Tiff watched him walk further into the forest and find another hide, one she hadn't seen before. From here, there was no line of sight into any of the chalets. She wondered if he was going to be up to that type of shenanigans today. What was the relationship with himself and Celia? It was another half hour of sitting on her bottom, watching a man do nothing inside a hide. Then when he emerged again, he seemed quite pleased with himself. This time he had a camera around his neck and Tiff continued to follow him.

She saw him take photographs of objects around him, sometimes of the trees, sometimes of a little scurrying animal off in the distance, but a half hour later he was back in the compound, returning into his chalet. Tiff stood at the edge, behind a tree. *That was a waste of time,* she thought. *Why was he out with his backpack?* It seemed to be quite a lot to take.

Tiff thought back to what Bertrand had done. She'd seen him the whole time, except for when he was in the hides. Had he genuinely just been going out to photograph the wildlife? Maybe she should check out the hides. Retracing her steps, Tiff made it to the first hide and stepped inside a small wooden construction. There was nothing inside except a bench. You could fit maybe two people at most inside one of these hides. It certainly had no warmth to it. Yes, if the wind were blowing hard, it would take away that element of the cold, but there was no heating, no fire. It was just a place to sit and watch the surroundings. You could see in two directions, so maybe it was located in a spot where wildlife would go past. Tiff had no idea—that was far from her speciality. Not that she couldn't work it out if she wanted to.

What would he do in here? Just simply look out? Surely, there was something else about these hides. That was always the thing, wasn't it, with investigations. Secret panels, but there were none in the walls. They were simply wooden, slatted, and there was no degree of thickness to be able to hide anything. Tiff stamped her feet up and down on the floor. *That sounded hollow, didn't it?* She went down on her knees in the cramped area.

It looked like a pile of dirt on the floor, but as she pushed back with her gloved hands, she saw that there were small planks of wood across the bottom. She tried to reach down and get her fingers into gaps to pull them up, but she wasn't able to. Reaching into her coat, Tiff pulled out a small Swiss Army knife. Taking the blade, she put it in between the gaps in the wood and the floor. Pushing back, she was able to prise up one edge. Getting her fingers underneath that edge, she was able to pull up a strip of wood. It had been a tight fit, so clearly there was a design in this.

She reached into the dark with her hand. Almost immediately, she felt something. Manoeuvring herself so she could see more of the floor, she reached down and took away two more bits of wood before identifying some packets in the void. There was a white powder inside them. It looked like drugs.

Carefully, Tiff lifted the packet out and unzipped the seal on it. She thought that there was an equivalent of a very small bag of flour, 250 grams, maybe. Maybe she should pocket it. No. If the drugs were gone, someone would know she'd been there. So instead, Tiff carefully placed them back. Somebody would come for these at some point, and maybe she'd be able to trace whoever it was back here. The one thing she knew was that Jodie had obviously been on drugs. Of the rest of the people in the compound, maybe the students were an option. She didn't see the family with the two boys being an option. And the Roberts didn't look like drug users. Maybe it was Denis; surely he must be on something, the way the man was acting? No, that was a joke. He was just a very strange little man.

Tiff decided to make her way to the next hide, to see if there was a similar situation. This time she ran most of the way to try to heat herself up. When she got there, she found the same slated wooden floor, but this time, the wood didn't lift. Tiff sat in the hide, wondering to herself. If drugs were involved, could they have been involved in the demise of Alice? Had she found them? Did she know anything about them? Was Alice taking them? People took drugs often at student parties. Maybe she took more than she was meant to. That was a reason people got killed, wasn't it?

The logical thing was to go and look at the hide near to there. Tiff made her way through the snow to the hide close to where Alice was found dead. Inside, she knelt down and lifted up the same slated wooden floor. This time it did lift. This time there was a space like in the first one, but there were no drugs. Tiff was feeling cold, so she decided to head back to the chalet. Maybe she'd see if Jodie knew anything about the drugs. The girl clearly was requiring some. Maybe this is where she'd gone that night. If she knew about the hides, maybe in her distressed state, she had thought about heading to them.

When Tiff strolled into the compound, she could see her aunt standing outside the students' chalet. She was talking to some guy, possibly Alan, the older one. Tiff stayed far away and made a wide route back to her own chalet. Taking off her snow boots once inside the door, Tiff hung up her coat and then entered the lounge area. Jodie wasn't there, and Tiff opened a flask to pour herself a hot drink. The fire was on, blazing well, and the chalet was warm. Tiff made her way over to her bedroom and knocked on the door.

'Jodie, are you there? I need to talk to you. Have you ever been out in the woods near the hides?'

There came no response. *Maybe she wasn't in the room,* thought Tiff. Opening the door, she saw the duvet lying over the girl, but her head was shaking slightly.

'Jodie. Jodie.' Looking at the floor, Tiff could see several bottles of alcohol, spirits. She quickly walked over to the bed. The girl was shaking. Tiff threw back the covers to see how she was, but underneath she saw just her bare back and buttocks. The girl was sweating profusely, clearly having a bad reaction. Throwing the covers back over her, Tiff wondered what to do. Keep her warm, give her water. That was it, wasn't it? Maybe Coralie would know what to do, or Cat. She needed to get somebody else in here, and quick. With that, Tiff walked to the front door, opened it up and saw Cat walking back.

'Jodie's got the shakes. She's in my bed. Get her some water. Keep her warm. I'm going to get Coralie, see if she's got anything we can give her.' Tiff looked at her aunt and she saw the slightly bleary eyes. It was a good job that somebody here could investigate sober.

Chapter 13

Maybe it was the air and stepping back out from the chalet that did it. That moment of standing talking to Alan and then making the short trip back to the chalet, but Cat was feeling a bit wobbly on her legs. Sure, she stopped drinking a while ago, but sometimes these things took time to hit you. She was a little groggy when Tiff emerged from the chalet, said something about Jodie, and made her way down to the main building for help. Cat forced herself forward, got inside the chalet, kicked off her shoes, dropped her coat, and made her way into the lounge. No one was there. She walked over to Tiff's bedroom; opening the door, she saw the girl lying shaking under a duvet.

'Not again. How much of that stuff do you take? What are you withdrawing from at the moment?' Then Cat looked at the floor and saw the empty bottles of booze. 'Have you had that down you as well? Blimey. Come on. We need to get you in the shower or something.'

'Not going anywhere,' said Jodie. 'Leave me alone. Let me be if you can't get me anything.'

Why do we have this girl in our chalet? Can't somebody else look after her? Cat was running out of patience. *I mean, the girl hardly helped herself, did she? Tiff could be a pain at times, but compared to Jodie, she was nothing. In fact, Tiff was quite a pleasant girl compared to Jodie. She really needed a good slap of life around the chops and be told to go and get a proper job, without needing an entourage to look after her. I'm royalty, and I don't need an entourage.*

Cat almost cursed herself. *I am not royalty, I'm just*—Then she stopped. Standing in the doorway looking at the shaking Jodie underneath the covers, Cat realized that she was doing it again. Taking charge. Getting on with things. Isn't that what the best of royalty did? When they run the country, wasn't that what they did? You put up with things. You go on with it. Making sure things didn't slide. Was that not royalty?

Of course, they look quite glamorous doing it and they had a lot of money. Well, she had a lot of money at the moment. Cat was never quite sure just how glamorous she looked. Glamorous to a student, though. He tried to make a pass, didn't he? But then again, she reckoned Alan would make a pass at anything—he seemed so desperate. He must be getting to that age, wondering if it was going to happen. The proper relationship, not the one where you mess about.

Cat had at least another five or six years before she would think about that sort of thing and it would involve family. *But I had a proper relationship with Luigi*, she thought. *That was proper. That could have ended in a family.* Who knew, maybe it was the drink, but a sudden depression came across her. *Come on Cat, pick yourself up. You've got a girl who's a mess in front of you and she needs to be dealt with before Tiff concocts some great scheme to sort her out.*

As she thought about what Tiff might do, the front door opened, and in marched her niece accompanied by Coralie.

'What have you done with Jodie?' asked Tiff. 'I think Coralie is going to be able to help.'

'Jodie's in there. You have a look, Coralie, and see what you think.'

Cat moved to one side, allowing Coralie to walk through. The ski instructor pulled the covers back and Cat reckoned that Jodie must be getting fed up with constantly being exposed and then covered back up again. Although what she could feel beyond the shaking, who knew?

'Go get her some water,' said Coralie. 'Let's get her to sit up in a chair somewhere. Contessa, have you got some clothes for her?'

'I haven't,' said Cat, 'but Tiff's should fit her. She has a bit less of a frame than me.'

'She's right,' said Tiff. 'I've got a good frame. Cat's a bit bigger.' Cat rolled her eyes at her, but Tiff was oblivious to what comment she had made. Once again, she was out in her own world saying it as she thought it was. Someday, Cat hoped, it would crash into her face. It would occur to her just exactly what she was saying to other people, but that was a vain hope. To think that was to not understand Tiff. To give her credit, Tiff was back in with a glass of water in no time, assisting Coralie in helping Jodie up. The girl looked wretched as they dressed her and moving her into the front room, they sat Jodie close to the fire in a chair with Tiff pushing water down her every five minutes.

'Just hydrate her. She's obviously needing something that's not alcohol.'

'You can say that again,' and Cat brought the two bottles out from the bedroom. 'I'm surprised she's still standing, although, she's not really, is she?'

'It's not much different to what you could handle,' said Tiff.

Cat saw Coralie's face almost in shock.

'That's not wine, Tiff. Those are spirits. Sorry, Tiff doesn't really understand alcohol. She doesn't drink.'

'Wise girl,' said Coralie. 'Jodie here would be a lesson to anyone. I don't think we want any fuss. I'll not tell Denis how she is because he'll flip the lid and he's up to high dough as it is.'

'That's a good idea,' said Cat and then put her arm around Coralie whispering in her ear, 'Do you think we can have a quiet word in the bedroom?'

Coralie nodded, took a look over her shoulder, and satisfied that Tiff had Jodie under control, she allowed Cat to lead her through to her bedroom. Cat waved her arm towards the bed allowing Coralie to sit on it, closed the door behind her and then perched herself on the desk at the wall. 'What have you found out?' asked Cat.

'It's not been easy. I have been busy with the power out. We've been running around dropping off the logs, making sure everybody's got enough, feeding people. I don't get to do the same walk around as you do. I have responsibilities.'

Cat nodded. 'That's fine, but have you found out anything?'

'Well, I went to the Plymouths, but they're not very forthcoming about themselves. I still don't know exactly what they do.'

'He's a musician, that I know, and he has a mum, brother, and sister but beyond that, I don't know much either.'

'Tiff said he had an eye for you though,' said Coralie. 'Maybe, you could use that. Maybe, you could get close to him and find out a bit more about them.'

Something inside Cat sprung up a hope, a flame but then she remembered her last adventure on a boat and the snake who had turned on her. The first officer who turned out to be simply a sleaze ball. 'Probably best if I don't. I'm not always the best judge towards a man I like.'

'Do you like him then?'

'Come on, take a look at him. I'm only a woman.'

Coralie laughed. 'I do know Gordon has been asking a lot of questions to Denis, all about the facility, where the power comes from, how things run, who else knows who is here, wealthy people booked up. Denis has been such a mess, but he's been blurting it out one way or another even though he's not meant to, confidentiality and that. Gordon has been very subtle, helping Denis, advising him, little bits in here, winning his confidence. Then Denis just spills the beans about everything. So unprofessional.' Coralie laid back on the bed putting her hands behind her head, 'I felt when I took this job that I might actually get somebody sensible running the place, you guys pay enough money. But look at him. He's so young.'

'He's probably my age,' said Cat.

'No,' said Coralie, 'he's not in his thirties.'

Cat almost swore. 'I think you'll find I'm actually in my mid-twenties. I might be an aunt, but that's only because my brother's a lot older.'

'Oh sorry, I just thought you were probably closer to my age.' Cat had one of those royalty moments where you simply smile. What she wanted to do was pick something up and throw it at this woman. When she was older, and people said she was older, Cat believed she could live with that, but being in her mid-twenties, she should at least be recognized as such. This was meant to be her prime, after all.

'Anyway,' said Cat, 'anything else you found out?'

'When I was over at the Roberts, dropping off the firewood,

they started off into a blazing row in the next room. I managed to get myself into the hallway, stand there and listen. I thought if I hung about in the lounge it would be a bit too obvious.'

'A row? What were they having a row over?'

'Who do you think? Bertrand. It appears he's not a first. Celia seems to be quite lively in the other men department.'

'Where are you from, Coralie? You've got a slight French accent, but you speak like a native?'

'Half cast. French father, English mother, but anyway, Celia has played around a lot; she's quite the girl, apparently.'

'Well, standing at windows, letting men photograph you,' said Cat. 'It's not something any girl would really want, is it?'

'When you get older, which obviously you aren't, maybe you'll find that things change or maybe they don't because you're right, most women wouldn't.'

'Did anything become of the row?'

'Oh yes, she hit him. She hit him, I think because he called her a whore, which I felt was pretty fair.'

'Darn right,' said Cat. 'I'd hit him if he called me that.'

'No, that's not what I mean. From the look of it, she's like some happy hooker.'

'Oh,' said Cat. She sat and thought for a moment. 'What's his buzz from her, though? Why is he still with her?'

'I don't know, I don't know where the money comes from in the relationship or maybe it's just the image, needing someone on your arm.'

'He did try to get his arm around me, very early on after I arrived, so maybe it's not a one-way thing.'

'Or maybe he's just frustrated,' said Coralie. The women seemed to be having a soft side for John Roberts. 'One thing I did find out, he's quite prone to going out on his own. The night Alice died, he wasn't in the house. Now apparently, he's here for the wildlife as well, but if you look at him and Bertrand, they're very different when they go out watching.'

'Yes, but Bertrand has been looking at a different sort of wildlife.'

'Yes, but he is very much the wildlife man. John Roberts disappears. He's got a coat on like he's going for a Sunday walk. He doesn't even take binoculars, half the time. There's one thing to go out and look at the wildlife around here. I've been there and seen it, but if you really want to get close to it, if you really want to understand it, you need to make use of the hides.'

'What's our next step?' asked Cat.

'I'm not sure,' pondered Coralie and there came a tap at the bedroom door.

Tiff stuck her head in. 'Are you two discussing the investigation without me?'

'It's not what it looks like, Tiff. Oh, actually, yes, it is. Is Jodie okay?'

'She's asleep, so if you don't mind, I'd like to join in because I found out something very important.'

'Come on in,' said Coralie. 'What is it?'

'Well, I trailed Bertrand out to the hides and in the bottom of them, there's a wooden fixture. It's like a floor. It's built out of strips of wood.'

'Yes. That's the way they're built,' said Coralie. 'I helped prepare a lot of them.'

'Obviously. Does the wood come up off the floor?' asked Tiff.

'They're secured down or they're meant to be. That's what you stand on. There's nothing underneath. It's just a floor to keep your feet off the cold ground.'

'No, it's not,' said Tiff. 'In two of the hides, I was able to open the floor up. There's a space underneath for storing things.'

'So, some of the hides are not in good repair,' said Cat. 'Big deal. Did Bertrand do anything?'

'No, he was looking at animals. He was checking for wildlife,' said Tiff. 'That's not the point. The important bit is that I was able to lift up these floorboards. There were things underneath.'

'How is that important?' asked Cat.

'Because there was a bag of drugs at the bottom.'

'You don't think you could have started with that? 'Hey, I found a bag of drugs.' That would have been a lot more helpful.'

'I'm just telling you exactly what happened. You need to wait, you need to hear everything properly. Don't have a go at me just because I'm making the breakthrough.'

'People have stashed drugs around here. I hardly think that's a major breakthrough,' said Cat. 'Look at the girl next door. I kind of noticed that there are drugs about.'

'Don't tell Denis,' said Coralie. 'He'll freak. They're not meant to have them here, according to the contracts. People are coming here with money. He knows what they've got with them. There was an entire sex party one night, up in one of the chalets. I heard it, I just stayed away, clear up wasn't great afterward.'

'Don't you see,' said Tiff. 'How important it is?'

'Not yet, Tiff,' said Cat. 'I don't. How is this important?'

'Because the two places that I was able to lift the floorboard of the hides, one of them was really close to where Alice was killed. I think she might have stumbled on it, stumbled on someone dealing the drugs.'

'Alice is, or at least she was, one of the more prudish ones from that group,' said Cat. 'That's one of the issues they have. Kyle was a real lad, drinker, everything, but Alice wasn't, and yet she fell for him. I wonder what she would have done if she'd found somebody dealing? Or maybe the person dealing doesn't want to be seen?'

'It's a bit elaborate though, isn't it, having the hides?' said Coralie. 'I mean, if you were just doing a bit of drug dealing. To go out and put it there, surely, it's got to be more significant than that? You said you found drugs, Tiff. How much?'

'I don't know what it was so, therefore, I couldn't put a value on it.'

'No, Tiff,' said Cat, 'she's asking the quantity, a wee bag, a big bag, what?'

'Oh. I thought it was like one of those small things of flour, 250 grams.'

'That's quite significant,' said Coralie. 'At least, I think it is. As far as I understood, when you took drugs, they all came in tiny packets, quite a small amount.'

'That's true,' said Cat, and then saw Tiff looking at her with accusing eyes. 'Hey, I've been to parties. I've seen things, okay. Doesn't mean I've done any of those. I never needed to take drugs.'

'No, you always had the drinks,' said Tiff.

'I'm not taking that from you. I'm your aunt—you watch your tongue.'

Tiff raised her nose to the air, and Cat could feel Coralie's embarrassment.

'Sorry,' said Cat. 'I do like my drink but I can handle it. But back to this. If it's a bigger amount, not a tiny one, you don't think somebody is actually doing some trading? You don't think somebody is actually here to swap stuff over?'

'It would give you more of a reason to kill, wouldn't it?' said Coralie. 'I mean, big deal if somebody's found a bit of drugs. Denis might be able to kick you out. With a bit of cash under the table, you probably wouldn't be going anywhere. Seems a bit extreme to kill for if all you had was a small bit. But if you were running drugs properly, that would be something, wouldn't it?'

'There's only one problem with that,' said Tiff. 'That would mean we'd have to have two drug dealers here making a switch, swapping things over. I haven't seen anybody that looks like a drug dealer, only people using.'

There came a clatter from the lounge. Tiff flung open the door, ran in, followed by the other two women. Jodie had stood up, the duvet had fallen off her and it looked like she tripped and was now sprawled on the floor.

'How long am I going to be here? I need something, get me down, take me down. I want to see Denis. Take me to see Denis. He needs to sort me out.'

Chapter 14

For an hour, all three women tried to calm Jodie down, but the girl was having none of it, tearing around the living room demanding Denis. In between bouts of rage, she would break down and cry screaming for her entourage, for those around her, and asking where they were. She would swear at people, tell them they weren't looking after her and then desperately clutch them, begging them to hold her.

'If she's going to go and see Denis, I think I better get down first,' said Coralie, 'because I'm not sure how he's going to handle it. We'll need to get him a game plan, some sort of structure, so he knows what he's doing. If she hits him, like this, blindsides him, he's liable to come up with anything.'

'Good idea,' said Cat. 'Why don't you go down and we'll be done in about five minutes with Jodie? Tiff can help me get her down. I'll tell Jodie she needs to freshen up a bit before she goes and sees him. Maybe I'll sit and do her hair.'

'You're obsessed with hair,' said Tiff. 'You think getting your hair done solves everything.'

'From the lady with the straightest hair ever. Enough, Tiff. It's just a way of keeping her quiet.' With that, Jodie stood up and started to scream.

'Go, Coralie,' said Cat. 'Tiff, get hold of her.' Five minutes later and after Cat had sat Jodie down and brushed her hair into a rough mess, improving it from an absolute mess, Jodie emerged from the house, one arm intertwined with Cat and the other with Tiff. It was beginning to get dark and through the gloom, the large fire in the main building was obvious. The Plymouths were down, eating at a table across from the fire. Cat could see Gordon Plymouth looking out of the window, watching the progress of the three women as they gingerly helped Jodie down from the chalet. The man was up and opening the door for them as they entered the main building.

'Are you okay there? You sure I can't be of any further assistance?'

'Thank you, Gordon,' said Cat, giving him a smile, 'but I think we'll take it from here. She just wants to see Denis. I think she's worried about her entourage.'

'Scumbags leaving me, just leaving me. Don't they know who pays them? Don't they know where the money comes from?'

'Easy,' said Cat, 'come on. We're going to see Denis. Over this way. We'll sit you down at a table. I'll try not to bring her too close to the kids,' whispered Cat.

Gordon smiled and Cat could feel him watching her as she made her way across a large room. With no one else in, the place seemed sparse and the bar was quiet, the students remaining in their chalet. Who knew what fight or tiffs were going on up there now. Part of Cat was glad not to be there, but she was also feeling somewhat tired. The alcohol had worn off, but she knew she had drunk it, her muscles saying that they should be in bed and not pulling some sort of victim like this from one building to another.

Coralie stuck her head from behind a door, talked to Jodie, Cat, and Tiff, and then shouted at Denis to come through. The man was practically hopping, all five feet, four of him, but he sat patiently in front of Jodie as she exploded with a tirade so loud that Cat insisted she kept the volume down. Cat stepped away, taking Tiff with her over to the fire, leaving Denis to talk to Jodie. It wasn't that there wouldn't be something said that she could pick up on; it was more of a case she was fed up with the woman and just wanted to sit down beside the fire. As soon as she did move, Cat noted that both Gordon and Julie got up from their table and came over to the fire to join her. The kids were running around the floor and after a rebuke from Gordon, they sat down to play some sort of clapping game with each other.

'She must be quite a handful for you,' said Julie. 'You've done very well with her. Those people who are with her normally, you couldn't pay me the money to do what they do.'

'They're probably parasites,' said Tiff. 'I've read about these clingers-on, just there to take the money off her. They probably don't care.'

'Another celebrity exposé from Tiff,' laughed Cat. 'You can't judge people too early.'

'You know I'm right. Just look at her, and you'll know I'm right.' With that, she turned her back.

'Is she all right?' asked Gordon. 'You seem to have offended her.'

'She's just Tiff,' said Cat. 'How are you two, anyway? Must be quite hard entertaining those two with the power out and that. I guess they want their telly, their games, or devices.'

'We've got a ton of snow,' said Julie. 'They'll play all day out there and they don't know what's happened. It's all a bit of an adventure for them. We've built a little tent for them inside the chalet, tipped the beds up and that. Don't tell Denis, I don't think he'll be too happy about it. Yes, they're very excited but they're also very tired, another half hour or so and we'll be taking them back, put them to bed for the night. It's just easier during the darker hours if they sleep.'

'Of course, it is, but I doubt you want to leave them anywhere at the moment.'

'Absolutely not,' said Julie. 'I think it was obvious to everyone that Alice's death was no accident. It does make you a little worried, doesn't it? But it will be the students; it will be her group of people. I don't think anybody else knows her.'

'You could be right,' said Cat, determined not to give anything away. Coralie's prompt to get close to Gordon to find out what he knew was still ringing around Cat's head, but she didn't trust herself. She also remembered how Gordon was asking Denis so many questions. Maybe they were just concerned, maybe they were worried, or maybe they had a part to play in this and they wanted to know if they had been found out. She needed to be careful. She couldn't just flirt around like she had previously—that had got her into trouble last time.

'What do you exactly do?' asked Gordon suddenly. 'I know you're a Contessa, but do you have a job?'

'My job is behind me there, warming herself at the fire. Tiff's quite special, quite brilliant at times, but she needs a lot of help with people, and with society, so I take care of her. I'm trying to travel with her, show her a bit of the world. I guess people would say I'm fortunate I've got the money to do it.'

'Yes,' said Julie, 'that must be a good thing.'

'You could say, but on the other hand, I did lose my husband.'

'That's right. Gordon said you were a widow. That must have been horrible. I mean, I got separated. Lucky escape, actually. It's funny, you can have kids with someone, and then realize just what they're like. It threw me for a while, but Gordon's looked after me, taking care of his big sis.' With that, Julie threw her arms around Gordon, hugging him tight.

They seem so normal, thought Cat. *Maybe that's the act. Maybe they're just good at this.* She couldn't work out how they would have anything to do with drugs. All the drug dealers she'd seen in films were nefarious people struggling to hold it together. These two were quite the double act. Raising her kids, seemingly getting on with life and dealing with it with aplomb.

'Are you okay up there, the three of you?' asked Gordon. 'It's just I know there's going to be quite a rough storm coming in tonight. I was talking to Denis earlier, and he's reckoning it's going to be another two or three days at least before they clear enough of the snow on the road away to get a vehicle up. By that time, it might be clear enough to get a helicopter here, but that's expensive. Still, with Jodie here, that might be what they do. I didn't realize how big a star she was. Denis says in Europe, she's massive. I have to be honest, I haven't heard much of her back in England.'

'Tiff knows her. Well, knows of her,' said Cat. 'I'm afraid I don't have that much of a scene anymore. I don't really keep up with popular culture.'

'Did someone say you had a bit of trouble recently on a vacation?' asked Gordon.

'Who told you that?' asked Cat.

'I'm not sure,' said Gordon. 'I think you heard it too, Julie, didn't you?'

'Yes. Someone said it. I don't know if it was Denis or not. That you were on a boat and someone killed themselves or got killed. That must have been difficult to deal with.'

'I wasn't really that involved,' said Cat. 'Just had to muddle through until the authorities got there. It was all a bit strange. A bit much. That's why I'm here. I was hoping to get away from it. It seems every time I go exclusive, that seems to bring a murder along with it.'

How did that get out? wondered Cat. She hadn't told anybody. Maybe Tiff had. She'd have to have a word with her. Maybe she was bragging about being a detective again.

'Anyway,' said Julie, 'best be getting the kids back up. You follow me up when you're ready, Gordon.' With that, Julie walked off, herding her two young children out of the door and up to the chalet. They giggled and shouted at each other as they left. Cat was glad of a happy moment amidst everything that was going on; the children's joy was refreshing.

'Quite a pair of nephews you've got there,' said Cat, 'you're very fortunate.'

'Well, you've got a niece as well, and you tell me she's bright. Life doesn't look that bad for you either.'

'Well, apart from the fact that the love of my life has died,' said Cat. She was being deliberately confrontational, but she saw straight away that she'd hurt the man with the comment.

'I'm sorry,' said Gordon. 'Insensitive of me. Of course, you're trying to get over it, aren't you? Trying to come to terms. Sorry, I shouldn't have said. I was just trying to—Yes, anyway, I'll leave you. I'll leave you alone, but please, anytime you want to talk or just have a few drinks or something or just come over and eat with us, you're more than welcome. I'll just go. Sorry.'

She watched the man walk away, shoulders slumped. If this

was an act, it was a darn good one. Maybe he just wanted to get to know her. Maybe he really was engaged, but she couldn't take the risk. As she watched him stroll away, something in Cat almost crumpled, almost wanted to chase after him. What was her problem? She always needed to have someone. She always needed someone close and frankly, at the moment, Tiff wasn't cutting it. Well, she couldn't, could she? There was that other side that you needed, not just the physical. It was almost spiritual, emotional. The sight of a lover that you really missed. *Anyway*, she thought and turned around to see Tiff warming her hands by the fire.

'Tiff, did you tell anyone about our previous trip on the boat, the one that went south?'

'No,' said Tiff. 'We talked about that before. Before we came here, you said, "Don't go around telling everyone you're a great detective," so I didn't. I do listen to you. You do realize that, don't you?'

'I do,' said Cat, 'but I've just been asked about it by Gordon and Julie and I'm wondering how they knew. You didn't drop it to Coralie, did you?' Tiff shook her head. 'I think there's something more to those two. It's all a big happy family act, but there's something else there.'

'Well, at least you haven't gone sweet on him,' said Tiff. 'Sometimes when I look at you, I see those eyes. I see the way you stare, and . . . oh my God, you have, haven't you?'

Cat immediately turned her head to see Gordon walking back to the chalet. Through the window it was dark and his figure was very indistinct, but clearly, her face had not been the mask she'd wanted it to be.

'Okay. Yes. He's nice. I like him, but he just came on to me and I turned him away. I learnt my lesson last time. I just hope if he's not involved, then I might be able to do something else afterwards, that I haven't just put him off for good.'

'That's the price of being a detective,' said Tiff. 'You got to focus on the job. You got to commit to it.'

'You're seriously lecturing me on how to investigate something? I think we're both amateurs here.'

Someone tapped Cat on the shoulder. Turning around, she saw Denis in a fluff.

'Excuse me. Excuse me, but please come over. She's getting very agitated and I think she needs something. I have some medication. Do you think I should give her it?'

'I'm not a doctor, Denis,' said Cat. 'I can't tell you what she can and can't have. You can offer it to her. It's up to her if she takes it. If you give her the medication, I'll make sure she doesn't drink. We certainly don't want them mixing.'

'No,' said Denis. 'That's a good idea. I will offer it to her.'

Before he could turn away, Cat took his wrist. 'Tell me, Denis, is the weather closing in? Gordon just said to me that it's going to be a rough night.'

'Very much so. Stay inside. Lock the door, build up the fire,' said Denis. 'I'm planning on going nowhere. I'm going to stay in here. Lock this place up and go to sleep.'

'I thought this place was meant to be open?'

Denis looked left and right in an almost comical fashion. Then, he lent in and whispered in Cat's ear, 'Don't tell anyone but I think Alice may have been murdered.'

Cat leaned in and whispered back in Denis's ear, 'I think you may be right.'

Chapter 15

'Are you going to be at that window all night?' asked Cat.

The women had brought Jodie back to the chalet, after receiving Denis's warning about the oncoming weather. They had allowed themselves to have dinner first, and having given a knowing nod to Coralie, they returned to their own chalet and locked it up for the night. Jodie was seemingly in a better mood. Whatever Denis had given her from the medicine cabinet, it had taken away the shakes. Although she wasn't quite ready to sit in a room with other people, she was at least sitting up in bed. Cat had made sure all the alcohol was put away because the last thing she needed, on top of whatever drugs Denis had given Jodie, was a dose of liquid that could send her crazy. The fire had been built up and the chalet was warm. As the wind started to pick up outside and the snow began to fall in a swirling fury, Cat was glad she was able to stretch out on a chair and simply relax. Yet Tiff was bothering her because Tiff was at the window with binoculars, staring constantly, flitting from here to there, looking at the other chalets.

'I doubt anybody is going to be doing anything tonight,' said Cat. 'Look at it out there—it's wild.'

'Best time to move. Best time to be hidden away and get things done. Can't be too careful with a killer about,' said Tiff.

Hark at her, thought Cat. *There she goes being the knowledgeable detective again. Say one thing for her. When she goes for a role, she really gets into it, even if she's half wrong about most of the stuff she says.* Actually, that was unfair. Tiff was clever, cleverer than Cat. Socially inept, but more intelligent. She could join the dots quicker than Cat ever could.

'Do you have to keep jumping about though? Come on, just sit down. Why don't the two of us have a night of it? We could do with some time off.'

'Never time off when there's a killer about.'

'Shush. Don't want Jodie to hear that. You could flip her over the edge.' Tiff looked slightly sheepish. *Well, at least that got through,* thought Cat. 'What can you see out there?'

'Not a lot, it's dark as well. I don't have any infrared binoculars. We must get some night visions. They'll be useful for us in the future.'

'Future? What do you mean, the future? I'm not up to solving crime on a professional level, making it my business.'

'No, but it might just be following us around,' said Tiff. 'When you've got a disposition like we have, or certainly like I have, it comes to you, doesn't it? It always came to the likes of Poirot and that.'

'He's a fictional character. Of course, it came to him; otherwise, there'd be no stories to write about in that book.'

'Yes, but some of us in real life are like that. I think I am.'

Cat let the matter drop and smiled to herself as she watched her niece intently gazing out the window. It was good to see her not just sitting with some earphones in, focusing on nothing. And they were working together, weren't they? She did feel she was getting closer to her niece, bit by bit. It wasn't easy, and certainly, Tiff would never admit it. Tiff saw herself as thoroughly independent, but if you ever pointed out the bits where she was not, she simply ignored you. Must be a great way to deal with life: pick out the bits you like, the rest of it, stuff it. Just shut down and walk away from it.

Cat wished she had been able to walk away from Luigi's death. At first, she had. At first, she seemed to have no problems. Yes, she missed him and she hurt, but not like she was now. It seemed that time had not been a healer; rather, it had been staving off this reaction that was coming to her now. Distraction, that had been the key, hadn't it? Taking herself elsewhere, finding the family, finding a new spot for herself, and then understanding what that was. Well, now, everything she'd been staving off was coming back at her. Poor Luigi. He'd been so pleased when he found her. Soulmates, runts of the family, that's how he'd describe them. Cat had laughed at him and teased him. 'Imagine calling the woman you want to love a runt,' but he was right. None of their family had wanted them and, in some ways, when they'd found each other, the family was happy. No longer would they have to do any looking about—they could just leave them in peace. Except for the fact that he died.

Cat stood up and walked over to the fridge. She had tried to keep it closed, but it had certainly lost its chill by now. Still, it was worth storing the water there, as it saved it from sitting around anywhere else. She opened a small bottle and drank from it.

'Throw me one of those as well,' said Tiff. Cat reached in, picked one up, and slung it across the room. It should have been an easy catch, and she saw Tiff initially looking at it, but something had caught the girl's eye, so instead of catching it, she turned and looked out the window. The bottle hit the wall just below the window, fell to the floor, fortunately, not splitting open.

'When somebody throws something to you, Tiff, you're meant to catch it, or make an effort.'

'Shush, I think he's on the move.'

'Who? Who's on the move?'

'Bertrand. It is him. Oh, he's dressed in black as usual, so he's blooming hard to see, but there's definitely movement in the snow. Come on, we need to get after him.'

'I'm not going out there,' said Cat. 'It's a howling blizzard. The man's probably just heard something at his door and popped out. He'll be back in, in a minute. You're not going to go animal spotting in this, are you?'

'He won't be animal spotting. He's up to no good. I'm telling you, he's our man.'

'Just because he's the one you were meant to look at does not mean that he's our man. He could be perfectly harmless out there. How do you know they're even his drugs? He was only in the hide. You don't know he put them there. You don't know if he dug them up.'

'But he keeps himself to himself,' said Tiff, running out into the hall.

Cat could hear her putting on her boots and she came inside, throwing Cat her coat. 'Come on, wrap yourself up in this,' said Tiff. 'Let's get going.'

'I am not going,' said Cat. 'It'll be crazy to go out there in this. If we get stuck, you could freeze to death.'

'Suit yourself,' said Tiff. 'I'm on it,' and she was gone. She didn't slam the door but closed it gently and she was gone.

Oh, hell, thought Cat and ran over to Tiff's bedroom, opening the door. Jodie was asleep. Upright, earphones still in, but fast asleep, tablet in front of her. *Oh, well, at least that's something.* She closed the door gently, put on her coat, and made her way into the hall. Putting on her snow boots, she then left via the front door and looked out into the darkness.

There was an occasional light from a chalet, the fire penetrating the darkness. There may have been a few torches inside, maybe even an occasional lantern, but the candles were running out and even when there had been plenty more, the chalets were barely lit. Up ahead in the distance, Cat could just about make out Tiff, her snowsuit a dashing yellow with blue running through it.

Cat didn't want to shout to her just in case Bertrand was within earshot and besides, in the howling wind, she wasn't sure how well she would be heard. She quickly made her way down the steps, running along until she joined Tiff at the edge of Bertrand's chalet.

'He's just gone through there, out into the woods. He's about one hundred metres ahead at most. Come on,' said Tiff.

Cat was hoping to catch her breath, but Tiff was away, and Cat ploughed after her. The hood on her coat came up, but she had no bobble hat on which would have made things a lot easier. There was no scarf either, and her face was cold as the snow was driven into it by the wind. Once they made the tree cover, the wind was not as fresh, and Cat felt she could pull the hood down despite the occasional bit of snow falling on her.

A hand was held up in front of her and she approached Tiff slowly. 'I think he's heard something,' said Tiff. 'He's looking around. Get down!'

With that, Tiff fell to the ground and Cat followed her. Catriona was unsure if this was just Tiff being dramatic or whether it was really warranted, but either way, she was taking no risks. Bertrand seemed a funny man, but he looked strong enough to be able to handle Cat, possibly Tiff as well. Of the two women, Tiff was probably stronger despite being younger, due to her slightly more energetic lifestyle. Apart from her strong swimming action, Cat was not the athletic type.

'He's on the move again,' said Tiff. 'Slowly, with me. Just stay behind me.'

It was quite something to see Tiff in this mode, up on her feet, directing things, feeling like she was fully in charge. Put her in a room full of people and she melted, unable to speak. Cat had no experience of creeping around, so she listened and followed Tiff's lead, although she was unsure where this experience of her niece was coming from. Soon, they saw Bertrand disappear inside a hide. He emerged five minutes later and as he disappeared off, Tiff ran inside.

'There's nothing there,' she said. 'That's the one I dug up earlier, the one where Alice died. There was nothing there. There's still nothing. Quick, let's get after him.'

The wind continued to blow as they made their way through the forest, and in the darkness, every loose tree and branch was a problem. Several times, Cat fell over, driving her chin at one point into the snow. She was fortunate that the worst she got was a bruised knee and she didn't have any time to think about it as Tiff hauled her to her feet, urging her on. By the time Bertrand had reached another hide, Tiff was already on her haunches watching him.

'This is the one the drugs were in,' said Tiff. 'But I don't get why he opened up the last one. Surely, he had known nothing was there. Unless someone was giving him a drop-off.'

'So now you've got him picking up the drugs,' said Cat. 'Can we make our mind up what's going on here? I thought you had suspected him of dropping them off.'

'Well, I don't know, do I? Let's just see what he's doing now.'

It was a few minutes later when Bertrand emerged again and walked back towards the women. Together, they huddled behind a tree, backs up tight against it, hoping that their breathing wouldn't be heard. *But then again in the wind,* thought Cat, *he's going to hear next to nothing.* They saw Bertrand disappear out of sight, and Cat followed Tiff into the hide. It was small, barely enough for one person, and so she stood at the door as Tiff reached down and started trying to lift up the floorboards using her penknife method. Cat watched as her niece groped down into the darkness underneath the floor of the hide.

'It was in here last time. No, there's nothing. It's gone. I reckon he's picked it up this time. He did have a backpack with him. Didn't he?'

Cat tried to think. 'Yes, he did. He did. He did have a backpack.'

'That will be where he's got them then,' said Tiff. 'So, he's picked up the drugs. Who's putting them out here, and how does that work?'

'What I don't get,' said Cat, 'is why these drugs are being dropped in different places at different times. If you were coming here for a meet, surely you'd drop them all in one go. Wouldn't you? Why is he picking them up all of a sudden, if he was there before picking them up when Alice came? Surely, you'd call off the drop. You wouldn't be putting more out. Would you?'

Tiff looked at her and somewhat amused, 'I don't know. All I know is there were drugs here and now they're gone. I know the other hide has a place where you can store them, and then they were lifted up again. Close to one of these places Alice was found dead.'

'We've got a killer amongst us, people creeping around in the worst of weather conditions. Anyway, we should get back. There's no point staying out in this cold and nonsense. Come on Tiff, replace the floor there and we'll get back. We'll see Coralie in the morning, talk through what we've seen. I don't think we've got anything to move with yet. We have to bring everybody on board with us if we say anything before the police arrive.'

'Okay,' said Tiff, and started replacing the floor. As they left the hide, Cat suddenly regretted leaving her hood down. She began to feel her hair become wet from the snow that was falling between the trees.

'I could do with my brush,' she said, and then she saw Tiff look at her. 'What? Okay, I could do with a brush.'

'I don't remember that in any of the books where the great detective stops to give their hair a brush. We're out here on business,' said Tiff. 'Try to be a bit more professional.'

'Professional?' said Cat. 'What do you mean professional? We're just a couple of rank amateurs thrown into this.' *What on earth does she think she's doing? As soon as the police get up that road, I'm handing everything over to them.*

The trip back to the chalet seemed longer than the trip out. Maybe because the adrenaline of following someone had gone. By the time they walked into the chalet, both were feeling tired.

'I think it's time to go to bed,' said Cat, 'otherwise, we'll not be fresh for the morning. I doubt anyone else is going to be out and about.'

'That's not a correct assumption, is it? I mean, Bertrand has already gone out, and he's taken the drugs,' said Cat.

'What else is out there to get?'

'I don't know, but you can never say never.'

'Fine,' said Cat. 'Get your binoculars, get onto that window, have a look. You tell me if anybody else goes out.' Tiff instantly picked up the binoculars and strolled across to the window. 'Who are you looking at?'

'Bertrand's house,' said Tiff.

'Anyone there?'

'No.'

'Okay, check the Roberts.'

'Anyone there?'

'No.'

'See, there's nobody about whatsoever.'

'I'm going to check the students.'

'Fine by me. Anything?'

'No, but hang on,' said Tiff. 'I think I can see something. I think Gordon's out,' she said. 'There's a figure down by the chalet, down at the Plymouth's chalet. Yes, somebody's moving about down there. I think it's Gordon, it must be Gordon, surely. What's he doing out and about?'

Cat's heart sank. Surely, he wasn't mixed up in this? She didn't want him to be; he was far too nice. But maybe that was it—he was far too nice.

'We can't let him just wander around,' said Tiff. 'We need to find out what he's up to. It could be an important part of the puzzle.'

'Or he could be struggling, being stuck in a chalet with two kids. Maybe he's just going for a bit of a night walk.'

'In this weather?' said Tiff. 'You said so yourself; come on.' Once again, Tiff shot out of the chalet.

How the heck do I get myself into these situations? thought Cat. *Do I really want to go? Do I really want to know what this guy's up to? Why can't they just be normal? Why can't they just be there to smile and enjoy a good holiday?* The front door of the chalet opened again.

'Come on; we're going to miss him,' said Tiff.

Cat looked around. She could still hear Jodie snoring, so she stepped into the hall and started searching the coat rack. There it was. 'Well, I'm certainly not doing this without a bobble hat,' she said, slapping it on her head as she stepped outside. She was sure, in most of the films, they went equipped with a firearm inside or some sort of secret weapon. Rarely did many step outside and feel confident of what they were going to do, armed only with a bobble hat.

Chapter 16

Cat pulled her bobble hat down, making sure it fully covered her ears and then tried to creep quietly up behind Tiff who was at the edge of the chalet, eyes focused into the dark.

'Where's he gone?' asked Cat.

'I think he's over at the students.'

'Is it him? Is it Gordon?'

'I don't know. I'm not that close, am I?' said Tiff. 'Come on. Let's see if we can get there. Whoever it is, they're at the front of the students' chalet so we'll come in from the back.' Tiff led Cat around the rear of their own chalet and then around the edge of the compound before dropping in behind the students' chalet.

'So, where is he?' asked Cat.

'He was out the front last sight. I don't know where he is now.'

'Well, you better find that quick,' said Cat. 'Otherwise, he could come around the corner of the chalet and find us, and then we're snooping as well as they are.' Cat watched Tiff walk quietly along the edge of the chalet. The wind was still whipping hard, so there was no chance of hearing where the person they were tailing was. Tiff turned around and pointed round the corner to Cat. Cat walked up delicately.

'He's listening in. I think there's something going on inside.' Cat put her ear up to a window, but the wind was howling, making it difficult to hear. She turned back to her niece. 'Do you think he's hearing anything as well?'

'I don't think so,' said Tiff. 'He's gone round to the front again. Come on.' Without waiting, Tiff then went down the side of the chalet, right to the corner. Cat could see her flicking her head around the corner briefly. When she caught up with Tiff, Cat received another signal pointing right around the corner from Tiff.

'He's just gone into the house. They've left the door open. Why on earth did they leave the door open?'

'Probably not enough keys,' said Cat. 'Especially with them coming and going.'

'Well, now we need to follow him in.'

'Hang on a minute,' said Cat. 'How are we going to follow him in? If he comes back out, then we walk right into him. There's nowhere to hide in there. Where are we going to hide?'

'Trust me,' said Tiff. 'I'll find somewhere,' and went to move off.

Cat grabbed her hand. 'No, you won't. You will not just walk in with no plan. You need to know where. We need to have something to say why we're in there.'

'Maybe we could say someone was walking about. That would be a good idea. We could say we were checking out to make sure everything was all right, because somebody was walking about.'

'So, us two women decided to just march right into the dark because someone's walking about in a place where we know there was a murderer about? We got some sort of death wish or something?'

'Well, we are right here,' said Tiff. 'You've just got to face the fear.'

There it was, another one of those throwaway lines. Cat was not sure that Tiff understood the seriousness of what they were doing. The murderer would surely kill again to cover up. The risks were very real. She wondered how Tiff's world was placed on top of this one. She didn't see things the same. Maybe Tiff thought she was in some sort of movie. Cat certainly did, but it was more like a horror film.

'We won't find out anything by staying here,' said Tiff. With that, she shook off Cat's hand and crept up to the door, pulling down the handle and opening it gingerly. Cat saw her peer inside and then a hand waved Cat to follow. Cat wanted to run, just get out of there. Keeping an eye on things at a distance was fine, but this was going to be incredibly close quarters if anyone came back.

Her niece was putting herself in trouble and she certainly couldn't explain her way out. Cat was the one with the silver tongue so, despite the fear that was running around in her stomach, Cat stepped forward and followed Tiff inside.

Cat knew if they opened the door ahead of them they'll be straight into a lounge area. The lurker, however, had gone ahead of them and clearly was through the door. The lounge area developed off to a kitchen and then to bedrooms. She doubted anyone else was up, and then there came a sound of someone moving in the room beyond the door.

'Tiff,' said, Cat in a whisper, 'quick, in behind these coats.' There was a coat rack hanging up on the side and the pair secreted themselves behind a number of overcoats and snow-jackets that were there. Cat thought they were reasonably well hidden, but if anyone went for a coat, they wouldn't stand a chance.

'So, stay hidden, stay quiet. We don't move from here unless we go back out of the front door,' said Cat. 'There's no chance of going in and staying undetected.' Cat felt she could hear her own breathing and tried to stop being so loud. Her heart was pounding, especially when there was another noise from inside and then there was a cry.

'You better sort it out. I didn't bring you all the way out here to do this. You said you'd get the money. You said it wouldn't be a problem—that's why we picked it. That's why we're here.'

It was a woman's voice. The man then replied, 'Stay calm. We'll be fine; it's all going to work out. I didn't touch her. If they come up, it's nothing to do with us—there's something else on the go; it must have been Kyle.'

'Don't you lie to me, Derek Lane, don't you lie. If you're up in your neck in this, you're not bringing me down with you. I only came out here to make some money just because father was daft enough to pay for it.'

It was obviously Debbie Ryan with Derek and Cat's heart beat faster as she heard the pair getting closer. But something else bothered her. Where had the other person gone if they were in that room? Clearly, Debbie and Derek weren't that far away.

'Anyway, I thought I heard someone snooping around earlier,' said Debbie. 'Go outside and have a look around; see if anyone is there.'

'I'm not going out in that weather, you've got to be joking. Besides, it will just look dodgier if I go. We've got to keep our heads down and we'll come out of this with the money. Besides, it's not our fault if Kyle and Alice go off on one. I can't believe he actually killed her though.'

'If it was him,' said Debbie. 'Anyhow, go outside to check for snoopers. The last thing we need is anybody poking their nose into our affairs.' The door from the lounge opened and Derek stepped out into the hallway. Cat started to shake as she realized he was reaching for a coat that was directly in front of her. She tried to edge slightly to one side. As the coat disappeared, she quickly brought her arm back inside.

'Are you seen?'

'Come here before you go outside.'

Maybe Derek would have seen, but Debbie had pulled him close. Cat could hear them kissing and then fumbling before the man started dressing in his coat. 'Check it's all clear,' said Debbie. 'Then we'll go to bed.'

'I'm not ready for bed. I can't sleep at the moment,' said Derek. 'Especially now I'm going to go out in the cold.'

'I didn't say we were going to sleep. Besides, I'll warm you up again. Go on. Hurry up. Make sure no one's out there. Best to be careful.'

Cat felt a hand touch her and nearly jumped before realizing it was Tiff's. She was starting to trace something on the back of her hand, but Cat couldn't make out what it was. Debbie stepped forward to the front door, holding it open while Derek went outside. For two minutes, the wind howled in and Cat felt the cold against her face as it rolled in beneath the massive coat she hid behind. Then the man was back and the door was shut. He was greeted with another kiss, and more murmurs of delight before his coat was placed back on the rack, right above Cat. It slipped down, and Cat instinctively tried to move to one side again. The man tried to hang it up three times before he just left it on the floor.

'Forget that,' said Debbie. 'Come on. Let's go have some fun.' With that, the pair disappeared. Cat gingerly reached across and took Tiff's hand, holding it tight. She then edged sideward and whispered in Tiff's ear, 'I think we should leave. If the other person comes out and they hear the door go, they might come down and search. We got lucky. It's a wonder they didn't see us here. If there hadn't been so many coats, we'd have been in trouble. This is a bad idea. We need to get back out and quick.'

'Agreed,' said Tiff, and went to move, but they heard the sound of the door opening. Cat froze. But her face wasn't covered. She could see the hallway. Anyone that looked at her would be able to see her too. Her heart thumped, but she dared not try to take cover in case she unsettled the coats or she gave away her position with movement. Tiff was obviously aware of what was happening because she squeezed Cat's hand tight.

Then a figure moved in front of her. It didn't look at her and the face was in profile. In the darkness, Cat could still make out the shape of a woman. The hair was obviously dark. It wasn't Debbie. But it was long. Yes, that was it. It was red; that's why it looked so dark. Slightly wavy as well. She had seen that somewhere, she had seen that on—it dawned on Cat. This was Julie. Gordon wasn't sneaking around. This was Julie, the mom of two. Why? Why was she watching everyone?

A part of Cat wanted to reach out, grab her, shake her and say, 'What are you doing?' Could she be the murderer? Why else was she stalking about? But then again, they were hiding, weren't they? Cat froze in her position staring ahead, praying that the woman wouldn't look around, but instead, Julie started to edge slowly along the hall. Cat could barely see her. Julie began to open the door and slipped quickly out. As sweat ran down Cat's face she began to shake. The tension that had welled up inside and desperately controlled, was now being released.

'Time to go,' said Tiff.

'No,' said Cat. 'She could be out there. We could open that door and walk straight into her. You have no idea what she's doing. We need to wait.'

There was a silence in the house that was only broken by a noise from upstairs as Cat stood there in the dark, sweat pouring down from her face. She could hear that Derek and Debbie were beginning to enjoy themselves upstairs. There wouldn't be any problems from this side of the house. For ten minutes, Cat stood still, her hand in Tiff's, before she finally decided to move.

Gingerly, she stepped out from under the coats, taking Tiff along. In the darkness, she fumbled along the hall, slowly turned the handle down to open the door gingerly before peering out. Everything was dark. This was it. She had to just take a chance, step out, and walk along. Carefully, she stepped out into the snow, Tiff following, and closing the door gently behind her.

'We go slowly, get ourselves back.'

Tiff nodded, and carefully they made their way to the end of the chalet. As they reached it, Cat thought she could hear something.

'I'm just going to peer around, check up the side,' she said to Tiff. 'You stay here and keep your eyes peeled, okay?' Carefully, Cat peered around the corner. There didn't seem to be anyone, so she rounded it and started walking up the side of the chalet.

The wind was howling and she couldn't see much, but there were footprints up the side of the chalet. Were they Tiff's?

Did they belong to her? Was she being fooled again by the snow? How long had they been inside? Thoughts swarmed through her mind, but she had no experience in this, no way of knowing which were their footprints and which were someone else's. She wasn't the spy with fieldcraft; she was just a young widow, desperately getting involved in something she probably shouldn't. Cat thought she heard something from around the other corner and continued up the side of the house slowly.

When she peered around, Cat could see nothing. Part of her wanted to have a torch, to shine her light, but then again, if this was the killer, would he—or maybe even she—hesitate if her torch was seen or would the killer just quietly dispose of her? Alice's neck had been broken and Cat reached up and touched her own neck. Rough way to go or maybe it was quick. Maybe this was one of those military people who could just snap necks like that.

A chill ran through Cat's mind. Best get back to Tiff. Take a chance. Leg it back to the chalet. Lock the door. If anyone had to get in, they could always press the button for Denis. He could raise everyone. Carefully, Cat walked back and made her way around to the front of the chalet. At first, she couldn't locate Tiff, looking here and there and then, until about twenty feet away, she saw her lying in the snow.

'Tiff,' Cat said out loud and ran over to her. Dropping down to her knees, she realized that Tiff was still warm, but her eyes were closed. Her chest was rising and falling, so she was still breathing.

It dawned too late on Cat. Someone must have been there. Somebody must have knocked Tiff out. Then somebody hit her on the back of the head with something else and everything went black.

Chapter 17

There was a pounding in Cat's head. The first thing she recognized was the fact that there was no cold in the air. The room was warm, extremely warm. In fact, it felt as if a fire was merely feet away. Cat realized she was lying on her front and she tried to push her arms down, to lift her head up. She blinked her eyes and there was a dancing orange colour. As the blur changed into a sharp focus, Cat realized there was a fire, several feet from her, a central pit with surrounding chairs, a sort of long settee, one that encircled the fire allowing you to face outwards from it. She'd always thought it was a bizarre design, but it seemed to work.

She was in the main building on the floor of the hall across from the bar, close to the burning centrepiece. Somebody had hit her, hit her hard on the head. Who dragged her here, deposited her in the main hall? Why? If she was a threat of some sort, surely the person would just leave the injured party, either that or finish her off. Had she been hit by Julie or had it been someone else? Was there another person creeping around that they hadn't noticed? She had constantly reminded Tiff that they were amateurs, and despite Tiff's protestations, it seemed that they were. *Oh heck, Tiff!*

Cat pushed out with her elbows, lifting herself up, and then rolled over onto her bottom. She was still groggy, but she looked around desperately and then saw the prone form of Tiff lying on the floor. She was on her back, eyes closed, but her chest was rising and falling, similar to how Cat had seen her out in the snow. *Thank God for that.* Carefully, Cat shuffled over towards her, on her bottom. She took Tiff's hand in her own, but there was nothing, no squeeze, nothing to indicate that Tiff knew Cat was holding it.

Cat looked around. The entire room was in darkness except for the light provided by the fire. Maybe Denis had gone to bed, as he had said he would. *But he said he'd lock up? Why then were they inside? Had it been Denis, but why? Why would he? The man was scared of losing his job. What possible reasons would he have had to have bumped off Alice?* Things were getting confusing, but at least Tiff was alive, and so was Cat for that matter. For a brief moment, she thought about Jodie, but Jodie could go hide. They'd all been in enough trouble. The key thing at the moment was that her niece was okay.

A sigh came from the kitchen. 'Tiff, wake up' and Cat got herself to her feet. She saw the candlelight coming through the window of the door that led through to the kitchen. Someone was there. 'Quickly!' She bent down and started to slap Tiff gently on the face.

'Go away, I'm not up for it today. No, I'm staying here.'

'Tiff, Tiff, wake up. Tiff, we need to move. Did you hear me? We need to move,' but Tiff continued to lie there. Fearing someone could come through at any minute, Cat grabbed both of Tiff's hands and dragged her along on her bottom to behind the bar area. Once there, Cat ducked down and not a moment too soon, as she heard the kitchen door close on its latch.

The footsteps came across the main hall and then someone

pulled out a chair and sat down at the table. Cat wondered if she should look, but how would she know if the person was looking at her?—she could give herself away. How would she explain where she was? It would all look strange. That was the trouble with snooping; if you got caught, you looked like the people you were trying to spy on. *There must be a better way to do this,* she thought. Someday she'd go to one of the experts and ask, she'd find out, but why? Why on earth would she do that? It wasn't like she was planning on getting into more of these scrapes. Once was bad enough, twice was just darn unlucky, three times would be careless.

Cat decided to crawl along behind the bar until she got to the end of it and peered carefully around the corner. Denis was side on to her and she watched as he carefully lifted a cup to his mouth, and took a sip before placing it back down. There was a tremor in the man's leg and he stared into the cup as if all the answers in the world lay in there. She thought the least he could do was put some liquor in it. That would have been Cat's solution, just knock a few things back. Well, you couldn't be classy all the time.

She dragged herself back and sat down listening to the rise and fall of the cup: up and slurped through the lips, then back down and the gentle tap on the table. This continued for five minutes and then Cat heard a rap on a window. Denis must have stood up because she heard the scrape of the chair as it went backwards. He muttered something under his breath, possibly a swear in French, and then he made his way over to the far side of the hall, the footsteps dying off gradually.

The door opened, then she heard him curse, this time in English, 'What do you want?'

'That's no way to treat a guest.' It was Debbie's voice. Cat wondered what the blonde was doing here. It brought back to mind her conversation with Derek; what had they been up to? What were they hiding? They were obviously close, but they're also in cahoots over something. Was Denis about to be an innocent victim? Cat dragged herself along the bar, again looking out from the side, but the fire was now in the way, in a direct line between herself and the door.

'Why are you here? You have caused nothing but trouble. One of your friends is dead and the power is cut deliberately. I know now it was deliberate. It's not down below—it's here, it's on the premises, and it's destroyed.'

'I don't know what you're talking about,' said Debbie. 'All I want is to pick up a few more bottles. We've run out; me and Derek are staying up tonight and there's no more wine left in the chalet. It is all-inclusive, isn't it? I can just go and help myself.'

Cat heard the footsteps coming over towards the bar, not the crisp sound of stilettos but rather the dull thud of boots. She panicked about what she would do if Debbie came behind the bar, she'd see them. How could she move Tiff?

'Wait,' said Denis. 'Are you telling me you had nothing to do with this? Are you trying to tell me that your arrival here and all this nonsense has got nothing to do with you? Even I knew it wasn't an accident. Someone in your group, someone had a problem with Alice. I think Kyle probably was the one. All the time in here, he's angry with her, shouting at her. They row and they row and they row. Then Alan, he stares at her with eyes while you're cuddling up to that Derek. He's not a nice man. The eyes, they're hiding something. Maybe he drinks too much. Maybe you both do.'

The tirade continued and Cat gently lifted herself up, peering over the top of the bar. Debbie had her back to her and she was blocking out the view of Denis. Carefully, Cat took a number of bottles of wine and slowly placed them on top of the bar. Maybe if Debbie found them, she wouldn't come behind the bar looking for them. She got one, two, three bottles up. Surely, she wouldn't be looking for any more than that. Then Debbie turned and Cat dropped straight down.

As Cat heard the footsteps walking over, her heart skipped a bit. She'd only put red up there. What were they wanting? White or rosé? Sparkling? Heck, champagne? No, champagne was all right. That was in the fridge further along. She could probably hang in tight, keep out of the way, not be seen if Debbie went to the fridge. If she was looking for the others, they were behind the bar, not chilled. The footsteps got closer. Then Cat heard them move to the side. This was it. She was coming round the bar.

'I still say it's you.' Denis had not stopped his tirade, and Cat heard the footsteps stop. Maybe she'd turned back again. Slowly, Cat raised herself. Debbie was slightly off to the left from where she'd been before. Cat moved herself across, getting Debbie in the eye line between herself and Denis. The man continued to accuse and slowly Cat continued to stockpile bottles on the bar.

She hoped the woman had had too much to drink, hoped she wouldn't be wondering how rosé and a couple of nice looking whites had appeared. It was only the matter of thirty seconds, but Cat let the bottles pass through her hand and then gently put them up on the bar at a speed she couldn't believe.

'Is there a problem?' The voice came from across the hall. Derek's voice.

'He's accusing us of all sorts of things—thinks we killed Alice.

Half blamed it on Kyle, then blamed it on me, said we were the cause of all the problems here. All I did was come down for some of the booze that he owes us. Up above his station, little caretaker. That's the problem. Man doesn't know when to hold his tongue. Well, my father's going to hear this; you bet he'll hear of this.'

'You won't be allowed back; you won't be allowed anywhere near here. When the police come, they'll sort you.' Denis was trying to sound impressive but the quiver in his voice was obvious. Cat held her fist tight, trying desperately not to make a sound, but then she saw Tiff's eyes open up. Desperately, she reached across, putting her hand across Tiff's mouth, pinning her to the floor. Then, fighting with Tiff as her niece began to struggle, Cat loomed right in front of Tiff with her eyes wide open, trying to telepathically encourage her niece to not resist and simply lie there.

'Listen, you little squirt. We're going to grab some booze and we're going to head back up to the chalet. Just get back to bed. You tell those police anything about us, you tell any lies, and I'll sort you. You understand me?'

For all that she didn't like Derek, Cat was hearing a new strain in his voice. It was hard, properly hard like a man who had said it before, and the threat was carrying weight. She heard Denis almost whimper before storming off. Debbie shouted after him that her father would hear of it. Then Cat heard her kiss Derek before some bottles were taken off the bar and the footsteps slowly moved away, back towards the exit to the chalets. All this time Tiff's eyes were wide, looking up at Cat. She dared not risk taking her hand off her niece's mouth. Who knows what Tiff would blurt out. Once the door was shut, Cat gently removed her hand, allowing Tiff to breathe easier.

'Where are we?' asked Tiff in a whisper. Cat raised a finger to her mouth, indicating Tiff should be quiet. Raising herself up, Cat looked around and saw again the dancing shadows of the fire racing around the walls of the hall. She couldn't hear Denis; maybe he'd gone off to bed. Maybe he had had enough. If she were him, she'd be back down with a key and locking up, especially after the threat that Derek had made. Someone was dead, after all. He couldn't take these threats as idle.

'How did we get here?' whispered Tiff in an even quieter voice. Cat shrugged her shoulders again, held up her finger to indicate quiet, and then motioned for Tiff to follow her. Slowly they crouched and walked around the back of the fire, shuffling towards the door to the chalets. Looking outside, Cat couldn't see anyone and she thought that Derek and Debbie by this time would be well up to their chalet and maybe even inside. Reaching the door, Cat gently pulled Tiff out and then shut it before stepping away.

'How did we get there?'

'In our chalet.' said Cat. 'Don't say anything else till we get to our chalet. I'll talk to you there.' Tiff nodded this time as if she comprehended the entire situation. Cat caught a view of Denis coming back from the kitchens, so she quickly pushed Tiff to one side of the door where there was no window and then breathed a sigh of relief once the door made a click. Denis had obviously locked it. He knew what was coming, knew the threat that was there, and at least they were both now outside.

'Do you have a lump on your head as well?' asked Tiff.

'Shush,' said Cat. 'Keep it quiet. I said when we get back up.' With that, Cat looked cautiously around the corner and through the window into the main hall. Denis had resumed his position at the table, staring into the cup. If he and his entire family were up for execution in the morning, he couldn't have looked more worried.

Cat routed the pair of them wide, right to the perimeter of the compound, before making her way up to the very top beyond her chalet. Then, approaching her chalet from behind, they carefully made their way back inside. As they stood in the hall taking off boots and jackets, Cat indicated that Tiff should listen.

'The thing is,' she whispered, 'Denis said that the power was cut deliberately. They didn't lose it down in the valley. It's been lost up here. Sabotaged deliberately.'

'Really? But to what purpose? What did that do for anyone?'

'What it did was keep people inside, or maybe it was supposed to, but there's a few people here that want to be outside. Remember, the drugs were in the hides around here. Maybe there's too much of a chance of somebody passing by. Even with cutting the power, look what happened with Alice. You might be right, Tiff. Maybe she stumbled on something.'

'Or we could have two very different things going on,' said Tiff. 'You always have to keep an open mind. Don't get too narrow, Cat.'

Cat sighed. She was ready for bed. Her head was still sore from where she'd been hit, and she was sure Tiff must have had a sore head as well. Still, if they locked the door, nothing else could happen until they got up. With that in mind, Cat made sure the door was double locked.

'I'm kind of glad you're going to be sleeping in my room,' Cat said to Tiff. 'It's good to have you to depend upon.' For a moment, she thought she saw her niece smile; she saw her niece take on board some of her aunt's anxieties.

Then Tiff said, ‘I actually prefer my own space.’

Chapter 18

With all she'd been through, Cat assumed she would simply fall asleep. If anything, she was too worried that in the morning she wouldn't get up, would miss something, but instead she found herself tossing and turning in the bed. On the far side of the king-size mattress, Tiff was out cold. She barely moved, with only an occasional snore to let Cat know that the girl was actually asleep and not dead. What it must be to have the ability to simply switch off. But then again, in Tiff's world, danger rarely looked the same as in Cat's.

Lying there, Cat initially stared at the ceiling trying to recall a memory that would lift her up, but every time she brought Luigi to mind, it just struck her that he was no longer around. In the end, rather than let the morbidity get to her, she rolled out of bed and made her way through to the bathroom, and splashed water on her face. Trying to keep as quiet as possible, lest she wake Jodie and have to contain another episode from her, Cat lit a candle and stared into the bathroom mirror.

Oh, those bags under the eyes. Well, that isn't surprising, is it? I haven't had a lot of sleep recently. With all that was going on, her hair was simply a mess. She tried to rotate so she could see in the mirror and find where the lump on the back of her head would be. All she had was a frankly disappointing mild bruise. Whoever hit her obviously knew what they were doing because it took one blow and she descended into darkness. Cat pondered on this.

The pair of them had been there prone and an easy target to finish off. It could not be the killer of Alice. They would have simply killed Cat and Tiff as well They would have seen them on the prowl. They knew they were hunting something down, but instead, the women had been dragged inside into safety. The attacker could not return them to the chalet because they knew Jodie was in there. Everyone knew that was where the little diva was locked up. So, they were taken somewhere safe, somewhere where someone could care for them. Maybe that was the point. Then Denis would find them and help them out. But Cat had woken up, and she'd hidden along with Tiff behind the bar.

Cat made her way into the lounge and took up a seat close to the fire. It certainly wasn't roaring. She threw a few logs on, trying to lift it again. *What should she do, read? Maybe a drink. No, no, that would be a bad idea.* She was not sure if the headache was from the blow to the head or from some of the alcohol she consumed previously. Maybe it was a mix of both. There wasn't that much alcohol left in the chalet, Jodie had seen to that. *Jodie,* thought Cat. *Why on earth did we end up with Jodie? Still, better have a look in on the girl.*

Opening Tiff's bedroom door, Cat looked in and found it difficult in the darkness to see the figure of their guest. Cat thought there was a lump there in the bed, but she was not sure, and made her way forward slowly, lest she scare the girl in some way. But as she got closer, Cat could not see a figure there at all and she reached out, touching the duvet, then grabbed the cover. Suddenly, she threw everything back, covers off, and saw an empty bed.

Cat flung open the curtains of the bedroom to find a day that was just starting to get going. *What time was it anyway?* The cloud hadn't lifted, creating a fog around the compound, but the snow was still lying thick, and it would be cold out there. *When did she go? How did she get out?* Thoughts raced through Cat's head. *Was it possible she could be somewhere for a sensible reason, or had she taken another turn and managed to get something inside her?* There were no bottles on the floor. *Had someone come in?* Cat had not been asleep. *But hold on, they hadn't checked Jodie when they'd came in. They'd gone off hunting Julie. They'd been bashed on the head, ended up in the main building, got themselves back, and they'd gone to bed. They hadn't checked on Jodie. She could have been out there for a while. Who knew where she was.*

Cat raced back to her own bedroom and started shaking Tiff.

'Get up. Jodie's missing. Jodie's missing.'

'Don't. I'm sleeping. Can you not see I'm sleeping?'

'I don't care if you're in a dream with Prince Charming. Get up, Tiff. Jodie is missing. We need to find her.'

'Why can't people just stay in bed? It's cold out there. It's nice and warm in here. We've been up most of the night, Cat. I'm going back to sleep.'

'The hell you are. Get up.' Cat reached down, grabbed Tiff's arm, and literally hauled her out of the bed.

'I might need a shower first.'

'Just get into your gear. Get changed, put a coat on, snow boots. Let's get out and find the girl. Where's that pager of Denis's? We need to get him up. We're not snooping around on our own for this one. We're going to gather people and go and find her. It's too risky on our own.' Cat got changed quickly, throwing on her snow trousers, a large jumper, and then putting her coat over her top and applying her bobble hat. She almost cursed herself when she had to tie up her hair without brushing it, but needs must come first—the girl was missing and they needed to find her.

She had to come back into the bedroom twice to haul Tiff into her clothes and then kick her out the door with her jacket and hat on. Staring down at the main building, she could see Denis stumbling about, unlocking the door, and starting to come up the hill towards their chalet.

'What is wrong?' he asked. 'What's the matter, Contessa?'

'Jodie's gone missing again.'

'Did you not lock the door?'

Cat took great offense at this. 'She's a grown woman. I can't just strap her in. She chooses what she's doing. She's a guest, not my prisoner, and I am not her nursemaid. But she's missing. We need to find her, Denis. You need to get people up. Get them together to meet outside the main building. We'll go find her.'

The man's face was pale and his arm began to shake. She put a supportive hand on his shoulder. 'Listen, Denis. It's important. You need to go and round everyone else up. We will search. We'll find her. Don't worry, we'll find her.'

'We need to find her. They'll be here. They'll say I lost her. They'll say it was me.'

'Get a grip.' Tiff was rather blunt, but something in Cat told her that the girl had now woken up and decided that this is part of what she wanted to do. When Tiff was focused, she was devastating. When she was unfocused, it was like moving the dead.

'I'll knock the students' door. You go over and get the Roberts, Denis. Cat, get down and wake up the Plymouths. I'll then try Bertrand, but he's probably wandering around, no doubt. We'll meet down outside the main building in five minutes. I'll brief everyone and we'll get right on with our search.'

Cat stepped back, almost impressed with her niece, but Tiff looked at her, 'I said you should go and get the Plymouths. Go.'

Suitably rebuked, Cat made her way then to the chalet nearest the main building, banging on the door loudly. 'Just a moment, just a moment,' came the call. The door swung open and Gordon Plymouth stood in his dressing gown with a large grin on his face as soon as he saw Cat.

'What's the matter? It's early; something happened?'

'You need to get changed, Gordon. You need to come with me. Jodie's missing. We need to go searching for her.' A face appeared over Gordon's shoulder. The long, red hair encompassed the face that looked tired. Cat recognized the bags that were under her own eyes and remembered how she'd seen Julie enter the students' house and then leave. This was the woman who probably knocked her out, or was it? Had somebody else been watching them? Somebody else had been careful to move them out of the way, but not harm them to any great extent.

'We'll need to find her, Gordon,' said Julie. 'We'll need to look for her. You stay with the kids, okay? I'll get changed. I'll go help them look, but we're not bringing the kids out into this.'

'Shouldn't Gordon come out?' said Cat. 'It's better if you stay as their mother.'

Cat watched the pair look at each other, less deciding about what was happening, more trying to explain why they were doing something. Cat found it hard to read their expressions, but they were clearly exchanging viewpoints without saying anything.

'No, I'll go,' said Julie. 'If anything's about, Gordon will be able better to protect the kids and I'll be safe in the crowd with the rest of you. Yes, I think for everyone's protection, it's best we work it that way.'

Gordon almost seemed surprised at the comment, but he nodded instantly, 'Yes, Julie's right, I'll take care of the kids.'

Cat stared at the smiling face of Gordon, searching into his eyes to see if there was something behind them, some deception going on, but she couldn't find any. She was surprised when he reached out with his hand, placing it on her shoulder.

'Don't worry, Julie will be useful. She's good at these things. I'll be fine here, but you take care of yourself. Please, take care out there. Stay close. Stay close to Julie.'

Cat smiled back. Once again, she was quite taken with the man, but danger bells rang in her head. She'd been down that path before. Why was he telling her to stay close to Julie? Julie herself had just said being in the crowd would be better for her protection. Yet Gordon seemed to be indicating that Julie would do the protecting. Cat was confused, but she smiled before turning away and walking to the main building.

'Take care.' It was Gordon's voice, and something about it sounded quite impassioned. Within fifteen minutes, a small party had gathered, ready to start searching the compound for Jodie, fresh from their chalets. Tiff insisted that the first place they wanted to start searching was the area around the compound, rather than any of the individual chalets themselves. Everyone was there, Bertrand, the Roberts, all the remaining students, everyone except the kids and Gordon. Tiff organized the party into three large groups. She would strike out with John Roberts, Coralie, Debbie and Alan. Sarah would go along with Denis, Derek and Kyle, while Julie and Cat would go with Bertrand and Celia. It was a good plan, Tiff mixing people up, keeping them in large groups.

Cat's group were sent out to the west and began walking along the perimeter through the woods. Given what had happened before, Tiff insisted that everyone check the hides; after all, Jodie had been found there before. Maybe she had extra drugs. Maybe she'd found alcohol that they didn't know was in the chalet. Maybe she was out of her mind. They had to make sure and not just assume the worst.

As the party started walking through the snow, Cat found Julie close beside her. She said little, but she could see the woman scanning here and there through the woods. At times, she would stop, check behind a particularly difficult place to see, kick the ground under things that Cat wouldn't have suspected. Little pockets that weren't within the eyesight, but you could tell something must've been there.

Bertrand stomped around at the front of the group. Now and then even he would mutter, complaining about this girl. Who was this diva and why was she out here? After all, he had bird spotting to do. Then Cat noticed that once they were clear of the main compound into the woods, Celia stuck close to Bertrand. She seemed almost unashamed. However, Bertrand kept trying to make a distance between them. He would come back occasionally, talk to Julie and Cat in the briefest of fashions, and then strike out on his own again, only to be joined by Celia. *Somebody doesn't want to be found out,* thought Cat. *Well, it's too late for that. Tiff's seen what he does with that camera.*

They came upon their first hide after twenty minutes of searching. Bertrand insisted on going in first. It took him only a moment to pop his head inside, and then the man walked away quickly and started into the snow.

'Something there?' Cat asked Bertrand. He simply nodded. Cat and Julie made their way quickly to the hide's entrance, peering inside into the dark. Cat saw Tiff's dressing gown and wearing it was the half-slumped figure of Jodie. The gown was half-open, leaving her in an indecent pose. Julie pushed in slightly in front of Cat, reached out, and touched the girl's neck. She then took her own hands and seemed to almost weigh the head with them before running the hands around her neck and across the shoulder area.

'Neck's broken,' said Julie. 'It doesn't look like an accident. Somebody go get Denis. He may not be the greatest caretaker everywhere, but he is in charge here. I'll stand guard.'

'I'll go find him,' said Bertrand. Celia instantly ran after him, leaving Cat with Julie. She wasn't sure how she felt about this. After all, she'd seen Julie the night before. Cat stepped away, keeping her distance but making sure she could see inside the tiny hide. Julie was another few minutes working around Jodie's body in some fashion before stepping out with a serious look on her face.

'Murdered. She was murdered. That neck's not been broken by accident. There's bruising where somebody's done it. As far as I can tell, she was murdered.'

Cat wanted to ask how she knew, wanted to probe her with questions. *Why was she out and about last night? What was she doing? Did she clonk Cat on the head or was she off doing something else? Where did she go after they lost track of her? Had Jodie been out at that point?*

'How cold is she?' asked Cat.

'Cold. It was done during the night.' That sent a chill down Cat's spine because Julie was out in the night, but so was Cat and so was Tiff and maybe other people were too. The pair remained silent, Cat keeping a distance of a few feet and never taking her eyes off Julie. She was delighted when she heard the approach of running feet. Denis arrived looking pale and ran straight into the hut. Tiff approached behind him with the rest of the group.

'Dear God,' said Denis, stepping back out of the hide. 'Dear God, she's dead. Don't blame me for this. She's dead. She's dead.' He seemed to look up to the sky briefly, and then the man simply collapsed onto the snow.

Chapter 19

The fire in the main building was warm, built up by Coralie after Tiff had ordered everyone back. They had brought Jodie's body with them, most of the party agreeing that it would be undignified to leave her in that state in the hut. Tiff had told Cat that she wanted her back for an entirely different reason, in case the murderer got a hold of the body and hid it. It was always harder to prove her death, even if everybody had seen it. They always wanted a body in the court. Cat wasn't sure if Tiff was right, but either way, she wasn't going to argue. Keeping everyone together and in sight was surely the best idea.

The only one missing from the main building was Gordon, as Julie had insisted that he stay with the kids. This bemused Cat because surely the kids' safety was no longer in doubt if everyone was in the main building. There was something about the woman. When they had been out in the snow searching, she looked like a professional. She saw nooks and crevices that Cat wouldn't have imagined, and she seemed to know where to search. There was almost a pattern to the way she walked. Cat had almost felt she could switch off and Julie would still have the ground covered.

Denis was sitting on a stool at the bar drinking a large brandy.

His face was still white, his hands shaking as he constantly muttered about his job and what they would do, how the press would blame him for the death of this young diva. Tiff, by contrast, was in her element. She had pulled everyone together, ordered Coralie to bring some soup out, and told everyone that they'd be asked to make an account of themselves before each other. It was almost like the end of an Agatha Christie, except Tiff hadn't done all the investigating first. Instead, she was offering a free-for-all, and Cat wasn't sure that was the best thing to do. The others seemed up for it and she could see the eyes staring across the room at each other, people wondering just who they had in the room with them.

There was plenty of alcohol flowing as well and no wonder people were nervous. Denis reckoned it would be at least another day, if not two, before anyone could get through to them, so it seemed they would have to do a bit of sleuthing on their own. They'd have to try to find the killer before he struck again.

'Right, everyone okay and ready to start?' Tiff stood up on the chair pointing at the gathered group, focusing them. 'If you don't mind, I think I'll start with an observation, get things going.'

Oh heck, thought Cat, *I know where this is going, she's going to set off the powder keg before it has even begun.*

'I've been following people recently, keeping an eye when I knew something was up and I trailed Bertrand the other day. He doesn't just like to watch animals. He has a camera and he likes to take photographs. The other day his camera was pointed at the Roberts's chalet.' Cat saw John Roberts cast a glance at his wife, who started to go red. 'It seems that Bertrand and Mrs. Roberts have an understanding, for he was taking provocative photographs of Mrs Roberts at the window, while Mr Roberts was out, of course. While this is an activity that they may want to enjoy themselves, I had an issue with it because the place he was taking the pictures from was right beside where Alice was killed. Were you taking photographs that day as well?'

'What are you on about?' said Bertrand. 'It was the middle of the night when Alice was killed. I was out photographing animals. I was photographing animals at that time as well.'

The man's skin colour had changed and he started to look slightly red. He was holding his voice, but he also was casting glances towards Celia who suddenly stepped forward.

'Yes, it's true. He was looking at me; of course, he was photographing me. Who would not want to? When you live in a marriage like mine, you have to take what you can get.' Behind her, John Roberts's face became like thunder.

'You hussy, you little tart. It's not like I didn't know but look at him. He's like the pervert you see at the back of a bookstore.'

'How dare you?' said Bertrand, stepping up to John Roberts. 'You'll pay for that, sir.' His fist was swung at Roberts who moved to one side and then immediately pushed Bertrand so he fell backwards onto the floor. As John went for him, Cat saw Julie reach forward and grab John by the shoulder. She seemed to have surprising strength and was able to pull the man back and push him away to a corner.

'Stop it,' said Julie. 'That helps no one. Maybe the man should answer the question. Where were you when Alice died, Bertrand? Were you there? Were you out in the woods at that spot?'

Bertrand pulled himself up off the floor, brushing himself down. 'Yes, I was out there, but not where she was. I was at the other hide, but I wasn't the only one in the woods. Ask Mr. Roberts.'

'That's true,' said Celia. 'I was at the window posing so John must have been out. I'd heard him go, though he'd never taken an interest in wildlife ever until this trip. What were you doing out there?' she spat at him.

'A man's got to have a hobby, especially when there's no entertainment at home.'

They are like two hissing snakes, Cat thought, *staring at each other, moving this way and that, but the real attack hasn't begun between them.* Bertrand was a sideshow, quite clearly for Celia. There was something long-rooted in this relationship and it was evil. It was bad to the core.

'Anyway, I wasn't the only one out there; those blasted students were there, too.'

'Who was?' said Debbie.

'Him for a start,' said John. 'That Derek guy. He was out and about.'

Everyone spun round to Derek, who was sitting beside the fire. Once again, the man's eyes looked shot, sitting back deep in the sockets, a pale shadow under each eye. He didn't simply look tired, he looked worn from things. 'I was out with Debbie getting a bit of quiet time to ourselves. Kyle will tell you; he saw us together.'

'Is that true?' asked Tiff. 'Did you see them out there?' Kyle nodded. 'And what were you doing?'

'Just looking for Alice—she wasn't in the house. We had rowed again. We were always rowing.'

'But where were you, Sarah?' asked Alan suddenly. 'I was the only one in the house. I was the only one stuck in that chalet. I know because I went looking for you. Where were you?'

Sarah Lyons went bright red and instantly looked over at Kyle.

'Plenty of night-time activities going on then,' said Tiff. 'But Jodie was out there for a reason. She was missing something,' said Tiff. 'I believe she was out looking for drugs.'

There was a sudden sound as a bar stool hit the floor and Denis had stood up.

'Listen, they cut the power. They destroyed the box up here. Someone did this beforehand, they planned it. One of you planned it.' With that, the man stood and stared, looking around him, sizing everyone up before Coralie came up and supported him on his shoulder. 'I don't trust none of you. I mean, none of you.' The man stumbled and Coralie put her hands underneath him, holding him up. 'I say you all go back. Take whatever provisions you need. Go back and lock yourself in your chalet and we wait. We wait the day or two days it takes for them to come here, and then we let them investigate. Let the police sort it out. Not this girl who is standing up like she is something. Dear God, and if any of you tell the papers about what's happened, I'll come for you. It's not my fault, you hear? It's not my fault.'

And with that, Denis stumbled forward, collapsing to the floor. Coralie ran over accompanied by Julie and then gently slapped his face before Denis came around.

'Just lie there,' said Julie. 'Stay there. Breathe. Just breathe.'

'He's right though, isn't he?' said John Roberts. 'We should stay in, safe.'

'Or we could stay here,' said Tiff. 'Here where everyone can watch each other. Stay in the room. There's a kitchen here. We can feed ourselves and we can stay here. People can be awake, two, three, four at a time.'

'No,' said Derek, 'I'm not sleeping in here with the rest of you. We go back. We lock ourselves away. It makes more sense.'

'Enough,' said Tiff. 'I've made my decision. We're all going to stay here.'

'And who made you the judge? You're just a girl,' said John Roberts. 'I'm going back to the chalet. Celia, grab some food. Need to have words with you, anyway. You've embarrassed me enough.' Cat saw Celia look over at Bertrand, but the man was shying away from her. Maybe he'd bitten off more than he could chew. The woman was disgusted, shook her head, and then marched off into the kitchen area. She could be heard banging about, packing things up, then came out with two large bags before joining her husband at the door of the building.

'Good idea,' said Derek. 'Come on, Debbie, Alan, the rest of you, get some food.' With that, most of the students made for the kitchen, but Derek went behind the bar and started stocking up with bottles.

'This is not good,' said Tiff. 'We shouldn't do this. Stay together, it's safer.'

'Looks like you've lost them,' said Julie. 'Don't mind bringing the kids and Gordon in here if you want. We can stay together as a group.'

'No.' said Denis, shaking. 'No, I'm staying with none of you, only Coralie. I know Coralie. I don't know any of the rest of you. Get your food and go. We wait it out.'

Cat looked at Tiff, who seemed to be almost ready to break into tears of frustration. She stood down from her chair and marched over to her aunt.

'Why are people so stupid? I had this sorted.'

'You didn't have it sorted, you just set it on fire,' said Cat, 'and now everyone's going to be locked away from each other. You need to learn to be more subtle with people. You can't impose your ideas, force them into things. Got to convince them it's their idea, but we are what we are. Maybe you should go and sort out some food.'

'Why?' said Tiff. 'You do it. You know what food is, you're better at it. Besides, I need to go and get my dressing gown back.'

'What?' said Cat. 'That's on Jodie.'

'Yes, and if the police arrive, they'll take it as evidence.'

'Tiff, it's the only thing she's got on. Enough. You don't need it. I'll buy you another one.'

'But that's mine. They shouldn't take it.'

'That's enough, Tiff. As your aunt, I'm telling you, that's enough. Go and get some food.'

'Okay,' said Tiff, 'but it's not over. We'll get to the bottom of this before the police arrive.' As Tiff walked away, Cat began to worry. *Just what did she mean by that? Are we going back out snooping again?* When she had organized the search party, Tiff had been sensible. There were plenty of people in large groups. Now, if they went outside the chalet, they'd be on their own together and this killer had struck twice.

'Are you okay?' said a voice. Cat turned around to find Julie staring at her. 'You're two women on your own. If you want, I can check up on you.'

'I don't think so,' said Cat. 'If we're going to play this, then we need to play it properly. We'll go lock ourselves in. Thank you for your concern.' Cat tried to read her eyes, but Julie just smiled and nodded.

'As you wish, but if you need us, just come down and bang on the door, and you're welcome to stay with us.' The woman walked off to the fridge and started taking out bottles of water and soft drinks, presumably for her kids. Cat looked around as the students began to leave. Bertrand was also stockpiling. Denis was having a towel waved in his face, a cooling breeze manufactured by Coralie. There was nobody here she could honestly say she could trust. No one here that Cat was sure was not involved. Well, only one person. She glanced over to the kitchen area and then saw her niece walk out back through the door.

'Peanut butter and bread all right for you?' she asked her aunt.

Chapter 20

The warmth of the fire made Cat curl her toes up, but it was good to be lying in front of it after the cold wash she had just had. With no power and no lights, she decided she couldn't wait to try to heat up enough water to make herself a bath. Instead, she washed quickly, flung on her dressing gown and moved the seat in front of the fire. Part of her was at peace. When they'd said for everyone to go back to the chalets, lock themselves in until the police arrived, part of Cat felt relieved. Tiff had put herself out there in danger, holding herself up as someone who would solve this, even if she had made a mess of it in front of people. That sort of challenge invites a disaster. It could invite the killer to come after her, but now, locked inside and awaiting rescue in a day or two, Cat felt at least her niece would be safe along with herself. The chalets were in full view of each other, and no doubt, like Tiff, many people were watching the windows seeing what anyone else was doing. But not Cat. Now was the time to relax. A time when, after all the strife, she could finally hand it over to someone else.

Tiff, however, seemed to be of a different vein. She had her binoculars and a seat by the window, and she hadn't moved in the last hour. It had taken them a good thirty minutes to get back to their chalet from the main building, chiefly because Cat had to re-enter the kitchen and pack up sensible things to eat for the next two days. She had also managed to acquire a small portable gas cooker, one used on treks for coffee by intrepid guests, so now they had hot drinks, could cook the odd hot piece of food if it were in a pan and plenty of other food to keep them sustained. There were candles and there were plenty of duvets, blankets, and firewood so that the cold would not get them. Yet Tiff was still restless.

From the moment they'd walked back into the chalet, Tiff had taken up her pew at the window, binoculars sweeping the vicinity. Anyone on the outside would have seen her there, knowing she was looking. Cat guessed if anyone did want to move about, they'd probably do it at night, and with that in mind, she made sure everything was locked up tight. The chalets had a couple of bars on the inside of the windows, meaning you couldn't open them easily. Cat intended at night time to block the door with several bits of furniture just to be safe. After all, there was a killer on the loose.

'Who do you think did it?' asked Tiff, not turning around from the window. 'I used to think it was Bertrand, but I'm not so sure now. But he still looks very suspicious.'

'You'd look suspicious as well if you were running out to take dirty photos of someone's wife, and besides, I just think he's a bit odd. You know she's not really into him, don't you?'

'Who?'

'Celia. Celia Roberts. She's not into him. She's just doing it to get at her husband.'

'Why?' asked Tiff.

'Because it's just the sort of thing they do. The marriage obviously isn't working. Something's gone sour, so she's hurting him. I think he likes to think that he owns her when, clearly, he doesn't. He's the businessman; he's the name on the money.'

'Well, if she's not interested in him, why doesn't she just leave?'

'It's not always that easy, Tiff,' said Cat. 'Sometimes there are other things holding you back.'

'Like what?' said Tiff.

'Well, maybe she needs the money he brings in, maybe she hasn't got a job of her own, maybe she likes the lifestyle, maybe he's got something on her. Who knows? She is outrageous though, dancing at that window. I wouldn't do that.'

'Even if Luigi had asked you?'

Cat went quiet for a minute. It was a moot question. Luigi wasn't like that; he wouldn't have made that sort of request. He'd have taken her off on some adventure somewhere. He might have danced with her before thousands in the streets of Venice, he might have jumped out of an aeroplane with her with a large parachute that said, 'I love you,' but he wasn't creepy like Bertrand.

'So, would you have?'

'He wouldn't have asked, Tiff. He wasn't like that.'

'But if he did?'

'Who's to say, Tiff, who's to say?' With that, Cat moved her feet closer to the fire, curling them up even tighter.

'I think it's one of the students,' said Tiff. 'I think it's a domestic in there. They seem very fractious, jumping around between each other, don't they?'

'That's true,' said Cat, stretching. 'But what did Jodie have to do with it all?'

'Wrong place, wrong time, maybe.'

'And what about the drugs, Tiff?'

'Well, that's what I was thinking as well. If somebody were worried about their drugs being hidden, or if somebody had found them, maybe they'd kill them. Drug runners don't shy away from killing people if they have to keep them quiet. Maybe somebody found them, maybe that was Jodie's problem. She found them.'

'I think it was more likely that she was using them and was in cahoots. One thing that does strike me,' said Cat, 'is that I find that Derek a bit strange.'

'Very,' said Tiff. 'He's not like the others, is he?'

'They said to me he wasn't from their course. He's not part of their group, really.'

'Did you see his eyes?' said Tiff. 'Very sunken, very withdrawn.'

'What did you say?' asked Cat.

'Withdrawn,' said Tiff, 'You know, like sunken.'

'Like Jodie was withdrawn. Do you think he's using?'

'Who knows?' said Tiff. 'What are they doing here, anyway?'

'Well, Debbie brought them. I told you this before.'

'But why choose here?' said Tiff. 'I'm here because of you. You chose here to get away from everything. I'm not sure it's really a student place. You'd think they'd be somewhere with a bit more nightlife, somewhere with people about, not stuck around here with depressed, lonely people like you.'

Subtle as a brick. Always subtle as a brick, that was Tiff. If you didn't know what she meant, she made sure you got it full bore and right in the face.

'I'm sorry if I don't entertain you,' said Cat. 'But you're right. I think Debbie's father paid for it. Debbie and Derek are pretty close, aren't they?'

'Totally. Maybe there's something going on there. Bertrand's on the move,' said Tiff, jumping out of her seat. 'He's all geared up in his black again, sunglasses on. This isn't daytime now. I don't understand how he sees anything.'

'Maybe he does, maybe they're only one-sided, maybe they're meant to make you think they're sunglasses, maybe he sees clearly. You can't see his eyes through them, can you? if you're perving about like him, maybe it suits him.'

'Anyway, he's on the move,' said Tiff, putting down the binoculars. 'Let's go see what he's up to.'

'What? What do you mean, let's go see what he's up to? We're staying in. The police are coming in a day or two.'

'Who knows who could be dead by then?' said Tiff.

'We're not in a TV drama here,' said Cat. 'There's two people dead. We have a chance to sit this out and let the pros take over. Sit down.'

'I thought that Luigi liked you because you liked adventure. You were different from the rest of the family, a bit like me really. Not so much as daring, but more like me. I'm going to solve this,' said Tiff 'and I'm nineteen, so you can't stop me.'

With that, Tiff barged out into the hallway, stomping into her snow shoes and grabbed her coat. As Cat made it to the coat rack, Tiff was pulling her bobble hat down on her head and opening the front door. 'If you're quick, we can do this together,' said Tiff, and shut the door behind her.

Damn it, damn it, damn it, what is she at? Cat stood and thought for a moment; there was no option here, was there? She had to go and find her, pull her back. Quickly, she put on her snow boots, threw on a coat, pulled the bobble hat down over her head, and stepped outside. The wind had picked up again and the snow was coming down in a flurry. She could see Tiff ahead, but she understood why she had the binoculars at the chalet. Figures were now getting indistinct at about three hundred yards. She would need to hurry.

Tiff had got up to the perimeter and Cat wasn't sure where Bertrand had gone, so she was unable to shorten the distance between them. Instead, she followed directly to where Tiff was, retracing her footsteps as her niece kept moving on. As Tiff reached the forest on the edge of the compound, Cat saw Tiff stop and quickly ran to catch up with her. As she approached, Tiff held up her hand and whispered.

'You need to keep it quiet. He might be able to hear you. He's used to being out and about in these woods. You're lucky the wind's coming down. Just follow my lead.'

Cat grabbed Tiff's shoulders, pulled her back, and whispered into her ear, 'Turn around, get back—we need to get back.'

'But he's obviously out here for a reason.'

'Yes, and the last time we were out here, somebody clonked us. We could have ended up dead. I'm not losing you, Tiff. Get back to the chalet.'

Tiff gave a shrug of her shoulders and moved off quickly forward. Cat struggled to keep up. When it came to it, Tiff was at least as strong as Cat. Yes, as her aunt, and having seven years on her, Cat was a larger shape, mainly because of how thin Tiff was, but Tiff was sinewy, there was muscle in there, and with her snowboarding activities, she was as fit as a fiddle. Cat, on the other hand, she might have had curves, but she didn't have the muscles. *Blast it,* she thought, *the least I can do is stay with her*. Cat raced off through the snow after her.

Bertrand seemed to be following his usual route. As they made their way through the wood, Cat was beginning to feel that she understood the layout properly. Once she got used to not looking at the trees, but at other things that were around, such as a different stump, the hides, other little paths cut away here and there, you began to orientate yourself far better, but she was very aware that with the low cloud, they were still only seeing several hundred yards ahead.

Cat nearly ran into Tiff as she stopped suddenly and moved behind a tree.

'He's going for one of the hides. I recognize his route. He'll cut into the right in a minute; the hide is just up there. Stay close, we'll come in from the other side.'

There it was; just as she had oriented herself in the forest, Tiff was going to take Cat off on a completely different route. The surprising thing was Tiff was getting good at this. The whole time they traced him, Bertrand had shown no signs of knowing he was being followed. Then Cat thought, *But we haven't even looked behind us either. How do we know we haven't been followed?*

Tiff was watching Bertrand. Other people surely may be watching as well. There wasn't a high level of trust going on at the moment, and if they believed that Bertrand wasn't the killer, maybe the killer would follow them. After all, Tiff had put herself up there as the promising detective. Peering over her shoulder, Cat looked out into the misty gloom. She saw nothing, and the wind through the trees took away any noise footsteps would have made. When she turned back, Tiff was already off and running.

Tiff was true to her word and managed to approach the hide from the rear. The lookouts were to the front, the door to the side, and so there was no way they could be seen. Once again Cat looked around. There was no one; maybe they would get away with this. Turning back, she watched as Tiff tiptoed slowly, carefully, up to the hide and lay up against it. She pulled down her hood and cocked her ear to the wall. Cat followed, pulling her hood down, fiddling with her hair for a moment, disgusted at how she hadn't brushed it after her wash, and then tried to listen intently.

'Does he know you're here?' It was Bertrand's voice.

'Of course, he knows I'm here,' said Celia. 'We were stuck in the chalet together. People were meant to be going nowhere. 'Oh, sorry, John, I'm just popping out to the toilet.' There's nothing I could say, I just went.'

'Good,' said Bertrand. 'Good. I'm glad I've got you alone.' The voices went quiet for a moment. Then they heard kissing, but it sounded to Cat that there wasn't a lot of conviction from one of the parties.

'What's wrong?' asked Bertrand.

'You know what's wrong. You know I can't leave him.'

'You know I can take you away from here.'

It was at this point that Cat realized that she was listening intently. Her entire focus was on what was going on inside the hide. Tiff, in front of her, was doing exactly the same. The joy of having two people is that someone can always watch the other one's back and the next time that they would be out and about, Cat would remind herself that somebody had to call who was doing this because right now, they were both fixated on the voices they heard and not on their surroundings. It was all brought into focus when a hand went onto Cat's shoulder, followed by another across her mouth. She tried to cry out, but it was a tight grip and an arm slipped around her neck.

Chapter 21

'I thought you were going to stay in your chalet,' a voice whispered in Cat's ear. 'I thought you were going to stay safe. It's not safe out here, is it? Your niece has her back to you. She doesn't even know I'm here. She doesn't even realize that her aunt could be dying right behind her and she'd never even hear.'

The voice was female, and Cat recognized it. It was the woman who had said to come and stay with her in the chalet. It was the sister of the man that Cat found so appealing. She had two little boys who played adorably in the snow, and here she was about to break Cat's neck. Cat went to struggle. The grip tightened, she couldn't move.

'Good job for you it's not me killing people, isn't it? I knocked you out the other day, took you back to the main building, but still, you insist on coming out. Why don't you let the professionals do this?'

Cat felt the arm releasing, but the hand stayed over the mouth. She turned slowly. Lifting her hands up in a sign of surrender, Cat found the hand on her mouth slowly being removed. She saw Julie's red hair and the woman was not smiling. Instead, she had a serious face on like she was scolding Cat.

'Sorry,' said Cat as quietly as she could. 'She just left. I couldn't leave her out here. I had to come with her.'

Tiff turned around suddenly and was about to shout when Julie raced forward, clamping her hand over her mouth.

'It's okay, Tiff,' whispered Cat. 'It's okay, she's, she's—actually, Julie, what are you?'

'Let's just say I worked for the organizations that keep your country safe before the kids, but you need to be listening in there. I think I know what's going on, but let's listen.' Julie leaned up against the hide, and Cat and Tiff followed her example.

'You know I can't leave,' said Celia. 'He won't let me. I'm tied to him. He doesn't mind me having a bit of fun; yes, he shouts, he complains, but he's sadistic. That's the sort of bastard he is. Let me have my fun, but never leave. He'd kill me if I tried, and he'd kill you too.'

'I can smuggle you away,' said Bertrand. 'We could go now. Head off down the mountainside. I could do that.'

'And go where?' said Celia. 'He'll always find me. You don't think he makes that money out of genuine business, do you? He's up here to see someone. I thought it was that girl, Jodie. She's smacked out as well. I've seen it. His business provides the top stuff. The stuff only the really rich can afford.'

'He was giving her drugs?' cried Bertrand.

'He wouldn't have,' said Celia, 'He doesn't do it like that, he watches from a distance. Somebody else here is working with him. Somebody else has contacts with her. He'd have told her who to look out for. Told her who to go to. That's why her entourage is away. She looked quite the junkie, and she certainly had the cash to buy what he was bringing in, but he doesn't deal with somebody else's minions; he deals straight to them through his go-to man. Someone here is his carrier.'

'I found stuff in the hides,' said Bertrand. 'The floors, they were loose, I picked them up and some had holes in them. Others, well, there were packets. I didn't touch them. You never know who it belongs to.'

'Quite wise,' said Celia. 'If you had taken it, he'd have killed you for it.'

'Did he kill Alice?'

'I don't know, do I? I was standing at that bloody window for you. He was out. It could've been him; it could've been anyone else. Half of those students were off their heads, I'm sure of it. But it's best if you just go, Bertrand. Go back and lock yourself in your chalet. When the police come, say nothing. Don't tell them about the drugs, don't say anything. You were birdwatching. Yes, tell them that you were looking at me, but nothing else. Nothing else and you'll live. Mention something beyond that, and then a week, a month, half a year, he'll come, he'll silence you. I've seen it before.'

Cat's heart was pumping. Pounding with excitement, shock, and adrenaline. So, the drugs were put here by John Roberts. John Roberts was the man doing this, but why was Alice dead? Surely, she had nothing to do with him, or was she his runner? And Jodie had gone out to meet Alice? But they said Alice was so straight-laced. That's why she was having the row. That's why Kyle was having problems with her. *The trouble with people is there's usually so many problems going on at once*, thought Cat. *So, who of the students was the mule? Who of the students was delivering the drugs to Jodie? Who was his contact for her? Surely it was Debbie. It was her father that was paying for this gig. Her father who had put them here. She would have had the choice. She would've made the decision. Alice must have found out, and she killed her. Maybe Jodie had gone off the rails. Who knew?*

Julie moved away from the hide, tapped Cat and Tiff on the shoulder, and indicated they should follow her. She stepped away and hid behind some trees some fifty yards away. As soon as they'd taken position, Bertrand left the hide. It was like Julie had known. She'd realized the conversation was coming to a stop, and she'd called what was going to happen next. Cat shivered in the cold, watching as Bertrand made his way back in the direction of the compound. Five minutes later, Celia set off in the same direction. Once Celia was clear, Julie snuck into the hide but came back quickly.

'There's nothing in there,' she said. 'No drugs. We need to find out exactly where John Roberts has been going. That way we can find the stash and hold it as evidence. Bertrand doesn't need to speak anymore. I've heard it. I can give the evidence but I need the drugs to confirm the story. Hopefully, get his prints on them. Hopefully, find the same drug inside Jodie.'

'But how is Alice involved?'

'I don't know,' said Julie. 'Not yet, but I need Celia. I need to understand what John's been doing.' Julie set off, waving at Cat and Tiff to follow her.

Celia had started towards the compound and so Julie seemed to be running in a straight line back, but they quickly caught up with Bertrand. He was still continuing his passage back to his chalet, but Celia had diverted, headed off in a different direction and Julie started to run round in a search pattern trying to find her. Tiff was keeping up fine, but Cat found herself puffing badly. She needed to get in shape. She needed to cut out the cocktails and get herself in shape. As Julie stopped to work out her next move, Cat almost collapsed behind her. This lifestyle, this chasing around after people, was too demanding. Luigi just liked her curves the way they were. She didn't need to be fit for him. If anything, she just had to learn how to lie side-by-side soaking up the sun together.

'Come on,' said Julie, and Cat watched Tiff take off beside the red-headed woman at a speed she knew she would struggle to keep up with. 'Oh heck,' she said. 'Let's go.' It took another five minutes to find Celia, who was wandering, tears streaming down her face. Even in the wood, the wind was cold and occasionally the snow fell down on your shoulders. It wasn't a good place to sit and cry but Cat guessed she couldn't go back to the chalet to do it or maybe she was taunting the man, giving him the idea that she was out for longer, up to other things rather than telling her impromptu lover to run and not come back.

'Fan out,' said Julie. 'Make sure she can't run away, we're going to need her help.'

With that, the three women spread right around Julie. She couldn't see them because she was crying, her head down, tears streaming off her face, dripping onto the ground.

'Are you all right, love?' asked Julie. 'You don't seem in a good way.'

Celia sniffed, a long drawn-out one, almost as if she were contemplating a response about seemingly being so broken up.

'I know. I overheard,' said Julie. 'I know what the tears are for. I think it's time you put an end to this. I think it's time you dobbed him in. You'll never be free of him. The Bertrands of this world will never be with you.'

'I don't want the Bertrands of this world,' said Celia, 'I just want to be me out there with no controlling hand on me. Not having to determine everything I do. Do you understand that?

Do you get it?' She turned to Cat.

'I get it exactly,' said Cat. 'It's time to stand up though, time not to be in fear.'

'He'll kill me. He'll kill me,' said Celia.

'No, he won't,' said Julie. 'I can put you away somewhere. I can get you a new life on the other side. My name's Julia, British Intelligence, and you're lucky because I'm actually on my day off.'

Chapter 22

Celia was in a mess. It was clear that Julie was putting pressure on her, keen to stop John, Celia's husband, from carrying out more drug deals and also to bring him to justice for what had happened. Of course, Cat realized, they weren't entirely sure what had happened. The assumption was that John, during his drug dealing, had been noticed, intercepted by Alice. Maybe he'd also been dealing drugs to Jodie when she'd reached the point where she was going to speak out against him. Whatever the actual issue was, it seemed there was no way Celia was going to testify against him.

'I get you're scared,' said Julie, 'but just tell me where he's been. Tell me what areas he's gone to so we can check these hides. I'm sure that's how he's doing it.'

'Tiff,' asked Cat, 'when you found the drugs underneath, you said they were like a 250-gram pack of flour. Is that right?' Tiff nodded.

'Wow,' said Julie. 'If that's the right stuff, that could be worth several hundreds of thousands of pounds, maybe more; it just depends what it is. I assume if Jodie was involved, it's top-notch stuff. It won't be the cheap stuff you get on the street. This will be brought in specially. They do that, they fly it in from foreign parts, usually from Asia. It's cut in some backwater somewhere. They bring it in, serve it up, make a fortune off it, but it only goes to the people who can afford it. Therefore, it has to go to the people at the top. People like Jodie, dumb enough to buy it, dumb enough to want it, rich enough to afford it.'

'Well, at least you're not dumb enough,' said Tiff, and Cat smiled. It was almost a compliment from her. 'I don't think you can blow that much on drink, can you?' Cat scowled. That was typical. Just when you thought she was coming in with a nice comment, Tiff would just blow it apart.

'Where's he headed off to recently, Celia? Which direction?'

'I only watched him once. No, maybe twice. He departed to the rear, up behind the Contessa's chalet into the woods in there. I think he walked round from that.'

'Well, he's clearly also been in the hides on this west side,' said Cat; 'after all, that's where Tiff found the drugs.'

'But the drugs aren't there anymore,' said Julie. 'If the most recent you've seen him head up to is the North, then we'll head that way as well. Check the hides up there. Are you staying with us, Celia?'

'I better head back. If I stay out and he sees Bertrand going back, he might think something's up. Something's wrong.'

'It's a good idea,' said Julie. 'Don't say anything to him. Try to avoid him. I know it's not easy within a chalet, but that'll be best until we come for him. It might take another day or two to get the real police up here.' As the women watched Celia head back towards her chalet, Julie took the girls to one side.

'Listen up, this could be dangerous. It might be best if you go back and stay in your chalet from now on. You've been extremely helpful and I'm sorry I sprung this on you. Maybe I should have been upfront earlier on, but I didn't know who to trust. Let me go and sort this out and then I'll come to you when everything's okay.'

'And leave you out here on your own?' said Cat. 'No. I won't hear of it. We're out here together now. We can always be on watch for you. Come on. Let's go find this.'

'That's right,' said Tiff. 'You're not taking all the credit. We were most of the way here before you even arrived. I've got a nose for this. You might have been on the job, but I'm a born natural.'

Cat rolled her eyes. 'It's not the time, Tiff. It's not the time. Let's just follow Julie. Give her a hand if we can.'

'Okay,' said Tiff and proceeded to march off ahead. Julie threw a glance at Cat. She shrugged her shoulders.

'It's the way she is. You just have to go with it.'

It took twenty minutes to walk round through the woods and then begin to cut across the northern part of it. There were a number of small hides and each one they checked did not have a removable floor. Cat could see the worry on Julie's face, but Tiff was happily marching on, regardless.

'Do you think something's up?' asked Cat.

'It's possible. Maybe Celia's double-played us. Maybe she's off already. I don't know. It can't be that much further to go. We've already come across two of the hides. There's usually only about three or four on each side as far as I understand.'

'Then maybe we better step up the pace,' said Cat, although inside she didn't like this idea at all. She was already struggling with the pace, but maybe it was the alcohol she'd drunk over the last couple of days that was dehydrating her. Either way, she knew this was an end game, so it was best if she carried on.

'Let's keep going,' said Julie, 'We'll be there soon enough.'

The next hide that they came across had a clear view of the compound. It was narrow, but if you stood in the right place, you could see one of the chalets. Cat wasn't sure, but she thought it might be her own. Thankfully, there were no windows there and maybe that was why Bertrand hadn't approached her asking for some sort of dancing favour. She couldn't get that thought out of her head. The sheer audacity of the man, lining up a camera as another man's wife danced for him. It wasn't so much kinky as just hilarious. Cat stood there looking through the small gap at her chalet and then heard a squeal of delight from Tiff.

'This one's got a bottom in it. It's here. We can open it up. Quick, Julie, have a look at this. Have a look.' Cat turned around and could see Julie's rear sticking out of the hide. Tiff must have been inside fully and a moment later Julie emerged holding a packet in her hand. Tiff had been right. It was like a small bag of flour. Carefully, Julie opened the packet with a small knife she produced from her pocket. She touched it with her finger, put it on the tip of her tongue.

'Well, I'm not completely sure what it is, but I think it's pure. He's definitely quite the businessman.'

'Do you think that will be it?' said Cat.

'No,' said Julie. We'll have to check the other one along here. After all, if Tiff found a packet before, and that has since moved on, it's being used. I think there's enough to start searching chalets once the police arrive. Somebody's got to be picking it up, using it.

'You mean somebody gave it to Jodie. Somebody separate?' said Tiff.

'That's exactly what I mean.'

'That's despicable,' said Cat.

'But profitable,' said Julie. 'Very profitable. But I'm not sure if the mule, the guy passing it on, is going to be a new person or not. Maybe that's why he's here. You wouldn't normally hang around. The other thing is, I wonder how much Jodie was buying. Was she testing it? She might have been bringing it all for her entourage. Who knows?'

'Whatever, we better get on to the other hide. People might start noticing we're not in. Especially if somebody tries our chalet door.'

'Or in case somebody actually saw you leave,' said Julie. 'That might be the real issue. Come on, let's get a move on.' The snow was still falling down hard in the gloom, despite the fact that the chalet could be seen. That was more an indication of how close this hide was, and by the time they reached the next one, the compound was again out of view. Cat had been dawdling at the back, struggling to keep up with the pace. Every now and again, she'd turn, looking over her shoulder. That was the thing about the woods, it felt like there was somebody there all the time. It felt like they were able to just pop in and out from behind trees. She had done it, hadn't she? Tiff and her. Admittedly, they had been following Bertrand, who didn't seem to be able to spot anyone, except for Celia, of course. He knew how to spot her.

Once again Tiff was up in the lead and she ran inside the hide as soon as they arrived there. Julie quickly followed her while Cat stood looking around, wondering if anybody was following. For a moment she thought she saw a shadow. Something out in the tree line, but no, it was nothing. Just the snow swirling around. She felt the breeze across the back of her neck, having blown her hair to one side. Cat took off her bobble hat, gave her hair a shake, started to try to smooth it into some sort of shape. It wasn't that she was bored, it's just this seemed to be panning out into nothing. That was a good thing. Lack of danger surely was always a good thing. Tiff would probably disagree. Cat wondered if Tiff really understood what danger was. Did she really understand that some of these people were dead, or did she think she was in a cop movie?

'Now, this is interesting,' said Julie, stepping out. This time she was holding a briefcase. It was metallic. She turned it over and over in her hands. Cat spied there was a numbered lock on it.

'What do you think's in there?' asked Cat.

'It's probably diamonds or something this time,' said Tiff. 'Maybe that's how they've been paying for it.'

'No, this is the mother lode,' said Julie. 'This will either be the main stash or it'll be where the cash has been hidden. Either way, we need to get it open. Hold on.'

She placed the case on the ground and produced what looked like a Swiss Army penknife from her pocket.

'What's that?' asked Tiff. 'I'm sure you can get those in the shop.'

'You can't get this in the shop,' said Julie. 'It's quite special and if you know how to use it, you can pick most locks with it but you just sometimes have to be careful. These cases can be booby-trapped.'

Cat watched Tiff take a step backwards. One, two, slowly backwards, and then two side steps to the left.

'If I thought you were in any danger, I would have told you to move.'

Tiff remained unconvinced and continued to step to the side. A few moments later, the lock sprung open and Julie carefully pushed back the lid of the case. Inside were numerous white bags.

'It's a test delivery for Jodie,' said Julie. 'Waiting to see what people can take. She must have been smacked out of her head.'

'Well, that's not really the most critical of observations, is it?' said Tiff. 'From the moment we saw her, Cat thought she was crackers.' Cat stared at Tiff. It really wasn't the moment for this. When Tiff went to speak again, Cat shook her head.

'Okay,' said Julie, 'we better close this and get back to the chalets. I can probably hide this before anyone else notices, but he may come for it. Although with the way things are, I think he'd be wiser to let it settle. Once the police have gone, then he'll move.'

'I think he's smarter than that,' said a voice. Cat heard a click. 'The safety's off, ladies, so don't try anything.'

'I take it it's a new delivery then,' said Julie. 'New batch coming into the country. Were you just using her?'

'No. Not by a long way. Jodie asked to be included. She financed some of it to get here. Awfully bad habit. Gets up to some silly things does that girl—or she did. A pity about her. She must have got in the way of someone.'

'She got in the way of you,' said Tiff.

'That's not true,' said John Roberts. 'The last thing I want to do is stop somebody who's paying me good money. I think she hounded someone else. Someone else broke their nerve.'

'Your mule, whoever was feeding it to her. You wouldn't have gone to her directly, would you?' said Julie. Cat saw John Roberts smile.

'Of course not, but I get the money back in.'

'Who is it?' asked Julie. 'Who's doing it? You may as well tell us. After all, you're not going to leave us alive out here, are you?'

'I'm not the killer but I might have to clean up,' said John. He moved closer, putting a gun into Cat's back. Cat saw Tiff react as if she was going to jump the man. She slowly held up her hand.

'Tiff, just stay calm. It's okay. He's just using me as a hostage.'

'No, he's not,' said Tiff. 'We know too much. He'll kill us all.'

'Right, clever girl. Now, be nice and quiet too. I think I'll put the three of you side by side.'

'Oi,' a shout came from the distance. While he kept the gun on Cat's back, John spun his head around to try to see who was there. 'What about my money?'

Chapter 23

'Stay back. You got paid. You don't need any more. You got the money you deserved. She's dead now. There's no more mark for you. All you have to do is shut your mouth.'

'Shut my mouth?' Cat recognized the voice. It was Derek Lime, Debbie Kimbell's boyfriend. It seemed to dawn on Cat now why he had the swollen eyes.

'I told you, you've had your money. Now you keep your mouth shut. Besides, you were taking some of the gear, that's evident. You've got the same eyes as Jodie.'

'There's something wrong with the gear, isn't there? It's not good. It causes things.'

'It gets you high. That's what it does,' said John. 'You think there's a side issue, do you? Does it make you a bit violent? It was you, wasn't it? It was you that finished Alice off. What happened? Did she see you?'

Derek Lyme had suddenly gone sheepish. 'It wasn't my fault. She came in when I was giving the gear to Jodie. She stepped into the hide. You see, she was like that, wasn't she? She's a bit of a prude. She'd hated Karl's drink. She hated it all. She told me she was going to go and see them. She was going to call it in. I just lost it. I just lost it. Broke her neck. Jodie never saw it. She was inches from me, but she never saw it. Smacked up so high, had no idea. It was in a moment. I snapped her neck in a moment.'

'I can't trust someone who tries the gear. You need to keep your head in this business, sunshine. You don't do something like that. You're done. You're lucky I'm letting you walk away from this.'

'You can forget that. I need the money. I've got debts. I can run more things for you. I can take it to other people. I've got connections. Debbie has connections. We know people. We can get places. You need to keep me in the loop.'

Cat felt the gun still wedged in her back, but the man had turned away and was watching Derek Lyme closely. 'You can forget it. Now be a good little boy and run back to your chalet and shut your mouth.'

Cat felt the gun go from her back. When she looked over her shoulder towards Derek, she saw him running towards John. A shot rang out, almost bursting her eardrums. Cat fell to the floor, but she heard Derek cry out. She turned and saw John turning the gun on her, but somebody was running at full pace and hit him, knocking him over to the floor. She saw Debbie trying to claw at his eyes, but the man was strong, throwing an elbow to her head before he tried to grab the gun again. Cat had barely moved, but Julie was on her feet and reached the gun at the same time as John. Cat watched him roll over and over and then the gun went off and a scream broke the air. Tiff grabbed Cat, pulling her away, and they began to run. As John got up, there was blood on his shoulder, but Julie wasn't moving. As they ducked behind a tree, Cat peered out quickly and saw John running in the opposite direction.

'He's making a break for it,' said Tiff. 'We've got to get him.'

'No,' said Cat. 'Julie can get him. Come on.' The pair ran towards her. When they got there, Cat saw Julie lying on the floor, her eyes closed, but she was breathing. She appeared to have been knocked out.

'Well, she's going to be no help,' said Tiff. 'Come on. We need to get him.'

'He's got a gun. He'll shoot us,' said Cat. 'Best thing is to be out of the way at the moment.'

'No,' said Tiff. 'We hunted him down, we found out who it is. We need to stop him. He's killed two people.'

'No, he didn't. The only people he might have killed are here now.' Cat stared around her. Derek was rolling about, obviously in pain. Debbie had been hit in the face and had blood running from her nose, and Julie was motionless. 'Derek killed two people,' said Cat, pointing at him. 'Or at least he killed one. I think he killed Jodie as well or maybe she just overdosed. I don't know. Anyway, John didn't kill anyone, so let him run.'

Tiff was away and Cat realized her niece was not coming back. Cat ran for all she was worth. She needed to get Tiff to slow her down to stop her acting. They couldn't be that far from the chalets, towards which John had begun to run. She knew where Tiff would be going, straight after him. Cat put everything she had into her legs as she ran as hard as she could through the thick snow. There was no way of hearing what was up ahead and John was out of sight, but she could just about make out Tiff.

Cat must have run for a good three minutes at full pelt before she broke the tree cover and found herself at the back of her own chalet. She looked left and right but saw no one. Tiff hadn't been that far ahead, had she? Quickly, Cat ran down the side of the house and came out near her front door. Again, she saw no one. Then a shot rang out. A log in the cabin splintered before another shot followed. Cat fell to the floor.

The man must have been at a distance. Where did the shots come from? She tried to crawl on her belly, to move towards her chalet and get around the corner to protect herself. Another shot blew out the window above her head. Cat kept as low to the ground as she could, but she thought she saw movement two chalets down. Maybe that's where he was. There was other movement as well. Denis had come to the windows of the main building, but when the shots had rung out again, he seemed to run away. The chalet on the east side had its door flung open and Cat saw Gordon emerge. When another shot rang out, he turned and ran back.

And then John Roberts came out from the side of the chalet. The shot had been good for the distance, barely missing Cat. But now he was walking over, straight towards her, the gun pointed. Cat went to stand up but the man fired and she fell down to the floor again. She was out in the open. She couldn't get round behind the chalet before he would get closer, close enough to shoot her. She'd have to stand. She'd have to run. There was no option. If she stayed where she was, he would get close enough and kill her.

Cat pushed up with her elbows, getting onto her knees before standing up to break into a full run. But she looked over her shoulder and her feet caught something and she fell back to the floor. He was less than fifty yards now and advancing at a pace. She tried to get up and stumbled again. She was going to be dead. She was going to be dead. She was going to be . . .

From the right side of her view, something came across and hit John Roberts in the head. It took Cat a moment to realize, but it was a snowboard. A snowboard with Tiff onboard. She had leapt into the air, coming at him with speed, and had caught him on the side of the head with the underside of the board. Cat watched as the pair collapsed in a heap, tumbling along.

Catriona stood up and began to run towards Tiff. *Where was the gun?* She screamed, 'Gordon' at the top of her voice hoping to get more attention, for someone to come, and then she saw John start to drag himself along the ground. Was he going for the gun?

Tiff was rolling around on the ground. She had come loose from her board and from where Cat was, she looked a little groggy, but if John got his hands on the gun, she was merely a few feet away. Cat ran as hard as she could and then she saw it, the black metal lying on the ground. John Roberts was only a couple of feet away from it. Cat ran as hard as she could.

When she saw him reach for it, rather than dive at it herself, she leapt, sticking her feet before her. She landed on her bottom, sliding hard along the hill, sweeping the gun away with her feet. Roberts reached out, grabbed her hair as she went past, and Cat screamed. She felt herself stop abruptly and the man had his hands on her face. He then reached around and grabbed her neck and began to choke her. Cat tried to scream again, but she couldn't. *Was this it? Could Tiff get away?* She wanted to shout for Gordon. She wanted Julie to be there. She wanted anyone to intervene, but there was no one. Just the man's face in front of her. He was snarling, his eyes livid with hate, his rage uncontrollable.

'Stop. Get up. Stop.' It was Tiff's voice.

John Roberts never flinched, continuing to throttle Catriona. 'Why should I stop? I'm going to kill this bitch once and for all. I'll kill you all.'

'Not if I kill you first. I'm trained in the use of firearms. I hope you know that.' Cat saw the man's face change quickly from that of rage to that of terror. He turned around, his hands still on Cat's throat, but he now saw Tiff. From her position, Cat guessed that Tiff wasn't bluffing, and slowly the man removed himself from Cat before standing up. Reaching for her throat, Cat coughed, struggling to regain her breath.

'You won't shoot me. You haven't got it in you. I'm going to come towards you. Your hands are going to shake and when they do, I'll lift the gun off you and then I'll turn you over to your aunt and side by side I'll blow the brains out of both of you. You see, I've done this before. I am in the business. I've disposed of plenty of people in my day. I don't always do it myself, but when I need to, I don't hesitate. You're hesitating with every second. You're wondering if I can just back down. Well, I won't. I won't back down. I will still be here, and you won't be, but you haven't got the guts to pull that trigger. Despite the fact there's no other logical option, you won't have the guts to do it. Think about it. What else can you do? What else?'

The sound of the shot ricocheted around the chalets and Cat watched the man flip forward and start crying out as he rolled around in the snow.

'Tiff, what have you done? What have you done?'

'He said the only logical solution was to shoot him, so I shot him.'

'You hit him in the knee.'

'It's my first gun. I was aiming for the head.'

Chapter 24

The snow had stopped, but the night was cold when the inspector opened up the door of the main building. It had taken several days for the avalanche to be cleared, but when they had heard the gunfire, they had put more men to it, worked harder, and eventually, they got a small team through. As he stepped inside the building, the scene before him looked comical. There were a number of people at the bar. One was mixing cocktails. Another, a black-haired lady of maybe around twenty-five, was downing them and had begun to sing. Beside her was standing a younger girl with straight hair and she was looking at a man whose knee was heavily strapped. The man was also tied to a chair. On the other side of him was the caretaker, a man the inspector recognized from a photograph he'd been given. There was a knife in his hand and the knife point was aimed at the man who was tied up. There was another man who had his hands tied, but he was being allowed to sit on a sofa and had a blonde-haired girl beside him.

A red-headed woman stepped forward, extending a hand to the inspector. 'My name's Julie Plymouth, sir. I'm with British Intelligence and if you'll come with me, I'll explain what's happened here.' The inspector looked up at her face and noticed she had a rather large bruise on her temple.

'Yes, it was pretty heavy going, but thanks to those two women over there, we seemed to get through.' The inspector glanced over and realized that the woman was pointing at the black-haired woman downing the cocktails and the rather focused younger girl with straight hair.

'And who would they be?'

'That's the contessa, Contessa Catriona Cullodena Monroe, who also happens to be one of the largest consumers of cocktails I've ever seen in my life. The girl beside her is her niece. Personally, I think the niece is more dangerous.'

* * *

Cat stood at the bottom of the slope, looking back up at what resembled a semi-cylindrical pipe. It was covered in snow or ice. Cat wasn't quite sure, and it seemed the most ridiculous shape to go charging down, but Tiff had assured her that Cat would be in the best position to see Tiff at her finest. As she prepared to watch, Cat felt herself shiver, but a pair of hands came around and pulled her close and she felt the warmth of another body.

'Do you put yourself out for her like this all the time?'

'It's hardly an imposition, Gordon, is it? This is Tiff's thing. I need to be here for her. Nobody else is. Nobody else cares.'

'She'd do the same for you, I guess,' said Gordon.

'Like hell, she would. Tiff's Tiff. Whatever Tiff is doing is the important thing. Nobody else. She saved my life by doing this. She clobbered him on the side of the head with her board. I'm looking forward to this.' She grabbed Gordon's arms, pulling them in tighter as she watched the small figure start to descend the pipe. At first, it went to one side, barely clearing it, before turning around and sliding the board up the other side. As the board took the air, the figure seemed to grab it, pulling it at an angle before turning and landing back down. It went to the other side, but this time, instead of grabbing the board, the figure rotated 360 degrees before coming back down. Again, it took to the air, this time 180 degrees before landing, going backwards. Again, it sailed up the pipe, but this time when it went to turn, the figure seemed to get lost in its motion. Suddenly all grace was gone.

Catriona raised her hands to her mouth as the figure crashed back down on the pipe, sliding along to one side, then down from that wall, eventually stopping somewhere in the middle. The board came off the figure's feet. It was thrown across the halfpipe and the figure turned and looked back up, shaking its head. The board was then reattached, and the figure slowly made its way down towards Cat. With an abrupt slide, a mere few feet from Cat, the figure stopped. The ski glasses were moved up to the top of the helmet, and gloves were thrown on the floor.

'What went wrong there?' asked Cat.

'Nothing went wrong. That thing is not symmetrical. That pipe is obviously shaped wrong.'

Cat shuffled slightly, so she was in the centre of the pipe looking straight up at it. 'Looks symmetrical to me.'

'Well, the angle must be wrong then. Something wrong with the angle. You wait and see. Coralie is coming down in a minute. It's all wrong. All wrong.'

A small figure started her descent at the top of the pipe. Like Tiff, the figure barely got up any height at the first side of the pipe, but by the time it had gone from side to side two or three times, it was flying to a height that Cat found breath-taking. More than that, each time it returned to the pipe, the figure landed perfectly and set itself up for another go. When it came out at the bottom of the pipe, having finished its run, the figure arrived and stopped a mere two feet from Cat before lifting up its goggles.

'That was fun. What happened to you, Tiff? I don't think you nailed that quite right. You seemed confused when you were going up.'

Tiff didn't look at Coralie. Instead, she looked back up at the pipe. 'It's not symmetrical though, is it? That's not symmetrical.'

'No, it was your entry into it. You were all wrong,' said Coralie.

'I've done it loads of times before,' said Tiff. 'I wasn't wrong. I've done this plenty of times. That pipe is not symmetrical.'

'It doesn't look like there's anything wrong with the pipe to me,' said Cat. 'It certainly looked fine for Coralie.'

'What would you know?' said Tiff. 'The pipe is not symmetrical.'

'I've been down this pipe millions of times. It's as symmetrical as you can get,' said Coralie. 'You went in wrong. You didn't come out right. It all fell apart.'

'It's not symmetrical,' said Tiff.

'It was symmetrical enough for me,' said Coralie, definitively.

Tiff turned, shook her hair. 'That's local knowledge for you. Any other pipe, you'd have fallen.'

Coralie walked off, shaking her head, and Tiff turned to Cat. 'She can't handle it, can she? She knows I'd be better. She knows ultimately I'd be better.'

Cat let go of Gordon's arms and stepped forward to embrace

Tiff in a large hug. 'You're the best. You saved my life. You're the best, but next time we'll leave it up to someone else.'

'Next time we'll be ready,' said Tiff. 'I want to learn to shoot.'

'Learn to shoot? You shot the man anyway. If you'd been trained to shoot, you'd have killed him.'

'Well, he just needs to learn not to mess with women like us, doesn't he?'

'Come on,' said Cat. 'We need to go and visit Julie in the hospital and you also have to drop by and make that police statement. Maybe it's best if you forget to mention you were trying to shoot him in the head. It's a good job you hit him in the knee, Tiff.'

'It's because I'm not trained. That's why it didn't work properly,' and off she stormed.

Cat turned around and put her hand out to Gordon. 'Come on,' she said. 'Let's go. Better go and see your sister in hospital.'

'Your niece, is she always right?'

'Only in her world,' said Cat. 'Only in her world. In her world, she's stunning. She's the best. She can do whatever she wants.'

'And in this world?' said Gordon.

'In this world, she's damn well lethal.' Cat laughed. Tiff was becoming the best fun she'd had since she lost her Count.

Read on to discover the Patrick Smythe series!

Start your Patrick Smythe journey here!

Patrick Smythe is a former Northern Irish policeman who

after suffering an amputation after a bomb blast, takes to the sea between the west coast of Scotland and his homeland to ply his trade as a private investigator. Join Paddy as he tries to work to his own ethics while knowing how to bend the rules he once enforced. Working from his beloved motorboat 'Craigantlet', Paddy decides to rescue a drug mule in this short story from the pen of G R Jordan.

Join G R Jordan's monthly newsletter about forthcoming releases and special writings for his tribe of avid readers and then receive your free Patrick Smythe short story.

Go to https://bit.ly/PatrickSmythe for your Patrick Smythe journey to start!

About the Author

GR Jordan is a self-published author who finally decided at forty that in order to have an enjoyable lifestyle, his creative beast within would have to be unleashed. His books mirror that conflict in life where acts of decency contend with self-promotion, goodness stares in horror at evil, and kindness blindsides us when we at our worst. Corrupting our world with his parade of wondrous and horrific characters, he highlights everyday tensions with fresh eyes whilst taking his methodical, intelligent mainstays on a roller-coaster ride of dilemmas, all the while suffering the banter of their provocative sidekicks.

A graduate of Loughborough University where he masqueraded as a chemical engineer but ultimately played American football, Gary had worked at changing the shape of cereal flakes and pulled a pallet truck for a living. Watching vegetables freeze at -40'C was another career highlight and he was also one of the Scottish Highlands "blind" air traffic controllers.

These days he has graduated to answering a telephone to people in trouble before telephoning other people to sort it out.

Having flirted with most places in the UK, he is now based in the Isle of Lewis in Scotland where his free time is spent between raising a young family with his wife, writing, figuring out how to work a loom and caring for a small flock of chickens. Luckily, his writing is influenced by his varied work and life experience as the chickens have not been the poetical inspiration he had hoped for!

You can connect with me on:

https://grjordan.com

https://facebook.com/carpetlessleprechaun

Subscribe to my newsletter:

https://bit.ly/PatrickSmythe

Also by G R Jordan

G R Jordan writes across multiple genres including crime, dark and action adventure fantasy, feel good fantasy, mystery thriller and horror fantasy. Below is a selection of his work. Whilst all books are available across online stores, signed copies are available at his personal shop.

Cobra's Fang: A Contessa Munroe Mystery #3

A robbery at the Contessa's highland home. The thief found dead at an island airfield. Can the Contessa and Tiff hunt the murderer across the continents and clear her deceased husband's name?

A visit home to the family residence in Scotland turns into a personal horror as the Contessa's private jewellery collection is ransacked. When the Cobra's Fang, a personal gift from her dead husband, Luigi, is found to be missing, Catriona, aided by Tiff, leaves no stone unturned in hunting down the culprits. But when Luigi's name is linked to an old gallery heist, Cat must travel the globe to clear his name.

Cobra's Fang is the third murder mystery involving the formidable and sometimes downright rude lady of leisure and her straight talking niece. When they spit on your husband the only reasonable course is to hit them with both barrels.

Destroy the family name and the Contessa bares her fangs!

The Satchel (Highlands & Islands Detective Book 11)
https://grjordan.com/product/the-satchel
A bag is found hanging on a lonely tree in an Inverness park. Inside, a morbid collection of fists tell a tale of murder and intrigue. Can Macleod find the killer and stop a second show of hands?

Battle-weary Macleod must seek to understand a murderer's obsession when a bag of appendages turns up in a local park. But as the links between the victims become more apparent, the possible identities of the killer increases. Can Macleod sift the wheat from the chaff and stop the killer before another bag is full?

Don't raise your hand if you know what's good for you!

Highlands and Islands Detective Thriller Series

https://grjordan.com/product/waters-edge

Join stalwart DI Macleod and his burgeoning new DC McGrath as they look into the darker side of the stunningly scenic and wilder parts of the north of Scotland. From the Black Isle to Lewis, from Mull to Harris and across to the small Isles, the Uists and Barra, this mismatched pairing follow murders, thieves and vengeful victims in an effort to restore tranquillity to the remoter parts of the land.

Be part of this tale of a surprise partnership amidst the foulest deeds and darkest souls who stalk this peaceful and most beautiful of lands, and you'll never see the Highlands the same way again

The Disappearance of Russell Hadleigh (Patrick Smythe Book 1)
https://grjordan.com/product/the-disappearance-of-russell-hadleigh
A retired judge fails to meet his golf partner. His wife calls for help while running a fantasy play ring. When Russians start co-opting into a fairly-traded clothing brand, can Paddy untangle the strands before the bodies start littering the golf course?

In his first full novel, Patrick Smythe, the single-armed former policeman, must infiltrate the golfing social scene to discover the fate of his client's husband. Assisted by a young starlet of the greens, Paddy tries to understand just who bears a grudge and who likes to play in the rough, culminating in a high stakes showdown where lives are hanging by the reaction of a moment. If you love pacey action, suspicious motives and devious characters, then Paddy Smythe operates amongst your kind of people.

Love is a matter of taste but money always demands more of its suitor.

Surface Tensions (Island Adventures Book 1)

https://grjordan.com/product/surface-tensions

Mermaids sighted near a Scottish island. A town exploding in anger and distrust. And Donald's got to get the sexiest fish in town, back in the water.

"Surface Tensions" is the first story in a series of Island adventures from the pen of G R Jordan. If you love comic moments, cosy adventures and light fantasy action, then you'll love these tales with a twist. Get the book that amazon readers said, "perfectly captures life in the Scottish Hebrides" and that explores "human nature at its best and worst".

Something's stirring the water!

Lightning Source UK Ltd.
Milton Keynes UK
UKHW040634200421
382290UK00001B/99